It was unbelievably *good...*

Now what? Addie was lying half-underneath Derek—instead of Kevin—and Derek was kissing her, sweet, perfect kisses that made her feel as if she was melting into the mattress. She wasn't exactly objecting.

Addie gasped. Derek had started tasting the curve where her shoulder left off and her neck began, sending shivers...everywhere.

She should either continue the seduction, or she could—and should—be honest: tell Derek she was sorry, but she'd made a terrible mistake. And then he'd stop sending her into orbit.

"Derek."

"Yes, Addie." He sounded amused. What was so funny?

"Um. The thing is."

"Ye-e-s?" He kissed her bare shoulder, a slow, gentle kiss that made her pause, because she wanted to enjoy it.

"I made a mistake."

"Really." He lowered his head to her breast; his mouth took her nipple. Wet heat. Pressure. A shock of pleasure through her.

"I thought you were Kevin."

Dear Reader,

The Maine coast is probably my favorite place on earth. The way the air smells, the huge ocean tides, the rugged rocky shores and thrilling wildlife—it always inspires me. And while I've never fallen in love there, it seems to me one of the most romantic places around.

My heroine, Addie Sewell, finds it romantic, too, when she attends the island wedding of a good friend. A creature of habit and routine, she is determined to get out of her rut by seducing an old crush. Instead, she is blasted out of her comfort zone by her first sight of sexy charter yacht captain Derek Bates, whose life spent wandering from port to port is about the last thing she could ever stomach.

I hope you enjoy reading about Addie's "wrong bed" adventures as she gets a whole lot more excitement than she expected...and maybe more than she can handle.

Cheers,

Isabel Sharpe

www.isabelsharpe.com

Half-Hitched

―

Isabel Sharpe

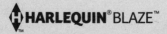

ISBN-13: 978-0-373-79765-3

HALF-HITCHED

Copyright © 2013 by Muna Shehadi Sill

HARLEQUIN®
www.Harlequin.com

Printed in U.S.A.

ABOUT THE AUTHOR

Isabel Sharpe was not born pen in hand like so many of her fellow writers. After she quit work to stay home with her firstborn son and nearly went out of her mind, she started writing. After more than thirty novels for Harlequin—along with another son—Isabel is more than happy with her choice these days. She loves hearing from readers. Write to her at www.isabelsharpe.com.

Books by Isabel Sharpe

HARLEQUIN BLAZE

To get the inside scoop on Harlequin Blaze and its talented writers, be sure to check out blazeauthors.com.

Other titles by this author available in ebook format.

To all the world's creatures of habit.

1

THE SOUND OF the ocean swelled through Addie Sewell's bedroom. She stirred in the soft cotton sheets and listened, picturing waves tumbling, sea foam forming lacy patterns that rushed in, then retreated across soft white sand. Somewhere far off a seagull called.

Addie groaned and threw off the covers on her twin bed. "Alarm off."

The ocean stopped. Or rather, the ocean sound stopped, made by her talking alarm clock, which she'd affectionately nicknamed Tick. The real ocean would have to wait until the following week, when she flew north to attend her friend Paul Bosson's wedding on his family's island in Maine.

She should be looking forward to this vacation a lot more. Been a while since she'd been anywhere except her parents' new house in Florida, and it would be great to see high school friends again. But honestly, she could use the time better staying home and going through boxes of old family photos and papers her great-aunt Grace had left behind, and to get serious about looking for a condo.

By living with her elderly aunt for two years before Grace's death, Addie had inherited this rent-controlled apartment a block from Central Park on Manhattan's E.

97th Street. With her actuary's salary, she'd saved enough for a down payment on the right condo. She just couldn't seem to find time or enthusiasm for the search.

To be honest, she was not a big fan of life changes, and the apartment was not only in a great location, but held lovely memories of Great-Aunt Grace.

Yawning, she stretched and blinked blearily at the freshly painted ceiling, a nice change from the crackling that had progressed for years. Desperate pleas to the landlord had finally been answered.

"Time."

"Seven o'clock," Tick replied.

Seven o'clock. Her eyes fluttered closed, shot open… closed again. Usually she had no trouble jumping out of bed in the morning, especially in the summer when it was so bright out. Lately it had become harder. Maybe she should get her iron checked. Or her vitamin D level. Or work out more.

The chime of an incoming text forced her eyes open again. Pretty early for anyone to be in touch. Mom and Dad were cruising the Mediterranean and her brother, Gabe, was off hiking somewhere in Nepal…

Anxious curiosity got her out of bed; she retrieved her phone from its charger and checked the message.

Oh, my. She was awake now. Wide-awake.

The message, seven words long, was not from her world-traveling family members, but from her childhood best friend Sarah Bosson, twin sister of Paul, next week's groom.

Kevin Ames will be at the wedding.

Kevin Ames.

Addie gave a short laugh, shaking her head. Look at her, all excited over something so silly. Kevin was two years older than Addie, Paul and Sarah, but he'd been on the cross-country team with Paul since middle school at John Witherspoon in Princeton, New Jersey. Addie and Sarah had seen him constantly at the Bossons' house. Last she heard, Kevin had some work conflict in Philly, where he lived, and couldn't make next week's Maine trip.

Ignoring her responsible side nagging that she should be in the shower by now, Addie texted back.

Since when?

Wow. She headed for the bathroom, still clutching the phone. Kevin Ames was The One That Got Away. Everybody had one. That person you never went out with that you really wanted to, or maybe you almost did, but something went wrong—the timing wasn't right, or, in Addie's case, when finally presented with the opportunity to start something with Kevin the summer before her senior year at Princeton High School, she'd totally messed it up.

Another text from Sarah:

He got someone else to go to his conference. Paul just found out.

Addie pressed her lips together to keep from grinning like a fool. She hadn't seen the guy in eleven years. He was undoubtedly married. In fact, she'd looked him up online several years back and yes, he was.

And guess what...he's single now!

Addie lost the battle with the smile. Okay, not married anymore. But that didn't mean anything. He could have put on four-hundred pounds, lost his hair and...

He's into marathons.

Oh. Four-hundred pounds was unlikely, then.
Well.
Addie shook herself. "Time."
"Seven-twenty."
Argh. She was behind on her morning schedule, which she'd developed specifically to avoid having to rush. From an early age her parents had modeled the importance of routines. Addie had scorned them in her rebellious— mildly rebellious—adolescence and her brother had no use for them at all, but she'd come to realize that routines could save you a lot of time and effort and trouble. You knew what to expect. You didn't have to think or make decisions, everything was already in the works and you simply stepped in and did your part.
Sarah again.

I told you about that jerk playboy Derek Bates being there? I so wish he wasn't coming.

Addie rolled her eyes. Sarah was pretty judgmental, but her anti-Derek rants were over the top, even for her. There was definitely something she wasn't telling.

Yes, you told me. But only about a million times. Gotta go to work. TTYL.

In her tiny apartment's tiny bathroom, Addie turned on the shower spray, counted to seventeen to make sure the water was hot enough and stepped into the iron claw-foot tub where she washed her hair and scrubbed up, thinking about…
Kevin Ames.
Who could help it? Not that he'd been all that remark-

able looking. Handsome, sure, but not striking. Bland all-American good looks, brown hair and eyes, straight teeth and an athlete's lean body. But he was so magnetic that women went nuts over him as if he were a knockout. Both Sarah and Addie had been smitten.

When Kevin Ames smiled at you, it was like no one else in the world existed.

Of course since Kevin was a really fun, friendly and popular guy, he smiled at a lot of people, including a lot of girls who were more beautiful and more stacked and more whatever-else guys found essential at that age. He'd always been big-brother sweet to Sarah and Addie, so they contented themselves with worshiping from afar.

Then that one August night, almost exactly eleven years ago, when Kevin was about to start his sophomore year at Brown, someone had told Addie that Kevin was interested in her. Addie couldn't remember who. But she sure remembered the feeling when he asked her out. Stunned, then euphoric, then terrified. She and Sarah had immediately started planning: clothes, makeup, attitude, everything he'd be sure to say and every way she should respond when he said it...

Get going, Addie.

She yanked the water off and dragged her towel briskly over her body. Back in her bedroom, she pulled on the clothes she'd ironed and laid out the previous evening, giving an exasperated groan when her first attempt at pulling on nylons ended in a run—and now she had no precious cushion of time left for disasters.

This was why she got up at the appointed hour every day and had everything prepared. Because she hated this flustered perspiring mess she got herself into when she deviated from the plan.

Great-Aunt Grace, her mother's aunt, had been even

worse—or better, depending on your perspective. Since she'd died, sometimes Addie went crazy, like she had cereal on Thursdays when Grace's cereal day was Friday.

She giggled, pulling on her black pumps. Wild woman!

The smile faded. She hadn't felt like a wild woman in a long, long time. Maybe never.

Kevin Ames.

The night of their date he'd picked her up in his gold Nissan sports car. He'd chatted easily with her beaming parents then they'd gone out for pizza on Nassau Street, and driven to Marquand Park, where she'd played as a child. Kevin had switched off the engine and produced a surprise fifth of vodka Addie had felt too intimidated to refuse, ignoring the voice that told her drinking was not a great idea for either of them.

At the fizzy height of her buzz, he'd taken her face in his hands, looked deeply into her eyes and kissed her.

Oh, that kiss...

She relived it until she realized she was standing on one foot, clutching her other shoe, and it was not getting any earlier.

"Time."

"Seven forty-five."

Eek!

Addie raced to the living room and snatched up her briefcase, stomach growling for breakfast she'd have to grab at work, headache demanding coffee. She let herself out of her apartment, snatched up the *New York Times,* which she usually read over breakfast, and ran down the hall, punched the button for the elevator, punched it twice more, as if that would do anything. Slowest elevator in Manhattan. While she waited, she checked her work schedule for the day.

Hey. She grinned at her phone. It was her half birthday. Addie Sewell was now officially twenty-nine and a half.

In another six months she'd be thirty. Still at the same job. Still living alone…

No, no, she *liked* living alone, loved the independence and the freedom. Though sometimes she wondered about venturing out to the humane society and adopting a cat. Cats were supposed to be good company, and more suitable for a small apartment or condo than a dog. Dogs were a lot of work.

The elevator doors opened to a good day getting better. *He* was in there, Mr. Gorgeous, the guy from the tenth floor, one of the most good-looking guys Addie had ever seen. In the three years she'd lived here, she'd never once had the guts to say anything more than hi.

So…she would again. "Hi."

Mr. Gorgeous nodded. "Hey."

The door closed, leaving that peculiarly charged silence in elevators that Addie tolerated with this guy because saying something and then relapsing to silence would be even more charged and peculiar. But if she started a conversation that lasted all the way to the first floor, then what, would they walk together into the street? What if he were talking to her only to be polite? Better not to say anything. So she stayed silent, watching the lighted numbers at the top of the door descend.

Kevin Ames.

He'd kissed her again, and again. His hand had traveled inside her top to stroke her breast, which felt wonderfully intimate and very hot. Except then Addie had started thinking about his last girlfriend, Jessica Menendez, and the size of her you-know-whats, and the girlfriend before that, Isabella Tramontina, and how she had a body that made men fall like dominoes when she walked down the hall.

Addie had compared them to her own pudgy small-chested big-butt body and virgin status, and panic had erupted. Was this all he wanted from her? To make out in a car drunk on vodka in a public park?

Then came the part that still had the power to bring the sick burn of humiliation to her stomach. Words slurring, she'd told Kevin she *loved* him. She'd told him she wanted their first time to be on a bed. But not just a bed. A bed of *white linen* strewn with *roses*.

Oh, God. She was blushing even now.

Addie would never forget the look of utter bewilderment on Kevin's face. He'd mumbled some kind of apology, said something about a misunderstanding, and had driven her home in a silence even more painful than the one on this slow, slow elevator. Kevin had gone back to Brown. Addie had gone back to high school. She'd heard about him now and then through Sarah or Paul, but hadn't run into him again.

Okay, for a few years, she ran *away* from him so as not to relive that mortification.

But she had enough self-confidence now to laugh about the incident with him when she saw him again next week. She was no longer a virgin and she no longer confused sex with love. Or at least she understood that for most guys they were separate entities.

The elevator door opened and she surged out ahead of Mr. Gorgeous so as not to burden either of them with forced contact.

On E. 53rd street at the offices of Hawthorn Brantley Insurance Company, she grabbed a bran muffin and cup of coffee from the cafeteria then met with teams to design a new life insurance plan and to work on storm damage models, then she formulated spreadsheets dealing with expected drunk driving deaths in Wisconsin the following year.

At lunchtime, back in the cafeteria, *New York Times*

crossword puzzle section tucked securely under her arm, she selected her usual sandwich, carrot sticks and apple, then threw caution to the wind and picked out a cookie. Special occasion! Her half birthday!

Eating the same thing every day meant she knew how many calories she was getting, and that they'd last through her workout and that she'd be healthily hungry for dinner.

Unfortunately she was a little late and her usual single table was taken. Heading for her second choice, Addie noticed Linda Persson, assistant director of Human Resources, seated by herself at a table for four. Linda was a lovely woman, but a little…well, she wasn't very attractive or very funny or very talented or very interesting, and at age sixty wasn't likely to become so.

Addie couldn't bear to see her sitting alone in her beige suit and ivory blouse, forking chef salad into her mouth, trying to look as if she'd chosen to be without a friend in the world because she so enjoyed the experience.

Sigh.

Addie put her tray down on the table. "Hi, Linda."

"Hey, Addie!" She smiled with such obvious relief that Addie banished the doomed feeling and put herself in the Glorious Martyr column.

"May I join you?"

"Of course." Linda pulled her tray toward herself as if there wasn't plenty of room already on the large table. "I was just thinking about my plans for the weekend."

"Fun ones?" Addie hoped they were special and interesting, because then she could think about something other than Kevin.

"I'm getting a new mattress Saturday afternoon. And then I'm going to see a movie." She pushed her too-large brown glasses up her nose. "I like going to movies by myself, do you?"

Addie nodded reluctantly. She did, but was ashamed not to want a lot in common with Linda. "I don't mind, either."

"I like getting there early because I like to sit in the middle of a row, not too close, and because I like to watch the previews, and have popcorn all to myself. And since no one talks to me, I can really disappear into the film."

"Same here." Actually…exactly the same.

"And then after the movie I'll probably go home and organize my kitchen. It's driving me crazy that the flour and sugar canisters are on the opposite side of the counter from the measuring cups and spoons. I've stood it this long, but no more." She tossed her mousy-brown curls, beaming triumphantly.

Addie took a long sip of skim milk to wash down her suddenly dry sandwich. She'd made similar changes after Great-Aunt Grace died.

"Sunday's my weekly brunch with my friend Marcy." Linda finished peeling a banana and took a bite. "We have sesame bagels with whitefish salad and read the *New York Times* travel section to plan fantasy vacations."

"Have you been on any?"

"No, no, they're just for fun."

"Why don't you go on one?" Addie was as surprised as Linda by the edge to her voice. She read plenty of travel articles, had the money and could take the time, but hadn't been anywhere, either. "Or two, or three or all of them?"

Linda shrugged. "I'm an armchair traveler. Saves me trouble and sunburn and storms and delayed flights."

Oh, dear. She forgot lost luggage.

"I'm a creature of habit I guess." Linda polished off her banana and picked up a brownie. "Like I have the same thing for lunch every day."

Addie stopped with a big bite of apple in her mouth.

"I feel comforted by routines. I like knowing what to expect."

Addie told herself to keep chewing, that she was never going to finish the apple while frozen in horror.

"I was thinking after work today I might stop by the humane society and look at cats."

Steady, Addie. She could panic, or she could take this lunch as a sign that maybe she was a tiny little bit stuck in a very small rut.

"They're supposed to be great company. Perfect for an apartment. And not as much work as a dog."

Large rut. Moon-crater-size rut.

Help.

Be rational. Rationality was one of Addie's best superpowers. She'd use it now, like this: it was good that Addie was faced with the person she could turn into. Especially today, her half birthday, because she had time to change before she turned thirty.

So she'd change. Starting today. Right after work, instead of going to the gym, then showering and having dinner in her apartment reading whatever parts of the *New York Times* she'd missed at breakfast and lunch like she did every evening—except when she had book group or dinner with a friend, she was going to…do something else. Like…

Well, she'd think of something.

She said a grateful goodbye to Linda and charged off to finish her day. By five-thirty, her plan had been cemented into action. After work she was going to Blackstone's on E. 55th. She'd have two drinks and look available. If nothing happened, one point for going and good for her, it was a start. If she talked to at least one guy, two points and a pat on the back. If she was asked for her phone number, three points and a high five.

Given that it was a hot sunny Thursday in late August,

when people were already looking ahead to the weekend, she'd give herself excellent odds on making two points and call it even on three.

Done.

Blackstone's was crowded and noisy, not usually her thing, but today exactly what she was looking for. She pushed her way into a spot at the long bar and managed to get a glass of Chardonnay from the bartender, thinking it might seem more feminine than the beer she was really in the mood for, and wondering if a navy skirt and cream blouse was any kind of come-on outfit. She was pretty sure it wasn't. But hey, Addie was alive and she was female. That was enough for plenty of guys.

She stood resolutely, sipping. Looking around. Smiling.

And sipping.

And looking around.

And smiling.

"Excuse me."

Addie turned hopefully to look into dynamite blue eyes. *Oh, my.*

"I was wondering." He quirked a dark brow. Even his eyebrows were sexy. "Is this seat next to you taken?"

"No." She tipped her head seductively. *Two points!* "Help yourself."

"Thanks." He didn't sit. But…his *girlfriend* did. Then the guy practically climbed into her lap and the two of them started sucking face.

Okay, then. Time to go.

She exited the bar, staggering into a guy as the alcohol kicked in. Did he catch her and did their eyes meet and did choirs of angels sing?

No. He said, "Hey, watch it, lightweight."

Right. Fine. Whatever. She'd go back home to her rut and stay there.

On the way she stopped into the supermarket on Lexington Avenue for a deli sandwich and a cupcake—chocolate with chocolate frosting.

Girl gone wild.

She made it home, hungry and cranky, managed a halfway nice smile for the doorman and stomped onto the elevator where she turned and saw Mr. Gorgeous coming into the lobby. Oh, just great. She rushed to push the button that would close the doors so she didn't have to face more man-failure, but she hit the wrong one and kept them open.

He got on. "Thanks."

"Sure."

The doors closed. They stood there in their customary silence. Addie took a deep breath. She had nothing to lose. Face it, she couldn't even see over the top of her rut.

"I'm Addie." She stuck out her hand. "I live on eight."

"Oh, yeah, right, hi, Addie." He couldn't have been friendlier, took her hand in his strong warm one. "I'm Mike. On ten."

She grinned. Maybe her rut wasn't quite so deep after all. "Nice to meet you, Mike."

"Same here." He looked her over, but not in a leering way, more polite and appreciative. "My great grandmother was named Addie. Not a name you hear a lot anymore."

"No." She wrinkled her nose. Men never associated her name with hot babes they'd lusted after their whole lives. Always great-aunts and grandmas. Addie's mom had named her after a Faulkner character in the novel *As I Lay Dying*.

So cheery.

"Any fun plans tonight, Mike?" Ha! Listen to her. No one could accuse her of being boring now. Maybe Mike would even like to split a cupcake.

"Yes." He nodded enthusiastically. "My boyfriend and I are going to make enchiladas and listen to *Madama Butterfly* live from the Met on Sirius radio."

Addie tried as hard as possible to keep her features

from freezing in dismay. Boyfriend. Of course. "That'll be great. It's a great opera."

Or so she assumed, not having heard a single note of it. "How about you?"

"Oh, well. I'm going to…" Sit around and cry until her hangover started. "Meet some friends. Later."

Like next week in Maine. Where Kevin would be. Though at this rate, he'd turn out to be gay, too.

Growl.

She escaped the elevator and let herself into her apartment, stalked to the living room and whapped the bag with the sandwich and cupcake down on the dining room table, not caring if one interfered with the other.

Let the celebration of her half birthday begin—alone with her take-out meal. And hey, after dinner, she'd meet up with Linda at the humane society and they could each buy eight cats and a truckload of kibble and litter and lock themselves into their apartments for the rest of time.

She got a big glass of water and opened the sandwich, wolfed it down and opened the cupcake to wolf that, too.

Her incoming text signal chimed. Addie put down the cupcake and dug out her phone. She could use good news. Maybe Sarah had some more.

Really glad you'll be there next week. Seems to me we have a lot of catching up to do. Maybe some unfinished business to attend to, as well?

Addie drew in a huge breath. Forget guys in bars. Forget Mr. Gorgeous. And definitely forget the cats.

Next week Addie Sewell was going to blast out of her rut and sail over the moon with The One That Got Away.

After eleven long years she'd finally get a do-over with her first love, Kevin Ames.

2

LAND HO. Derek stood at the front of the Bossons' forty-two-foot cabin cruiser, *Lucky,* as she made her way from Machias to Storness Island, which Paul's family had owned since the 1940s. First boat Derek had been on besides his own in a long time…seven years? Eight? Being a passenger felt strange. Or maybe it was the jet lag from the fifteen hours of travel, Honolulu to Portland, and the five-hour drive that morning, Portland to Machias, to meet Paul.

Lucky left the chop of open sea and purred into the protected cove on the island's north side, a mile from the mainland. Derek had visited the Bossons here only once, several years earlier, but the place was as picturesque and familiar as if he'd just left. The cove boasted a sand beach—unusual along Down east Maine's rocky coast—with the same driftwood branch he remembered lying across it. The white boathouse still stood among the birch, spruce and firs, its doors padlocked. Birds darted over the rocks on the cove's other side. Peaceful. Remote. Hard to imagine any of the world's constant turmoil still existed. Same way he felt leaving civilization and taking to the sea on *Joie de Vivre,* the eighty-foot yacht in which he'd invested—his parents would say wasted—a good chunk of his inheritance from Grandma and Grandpa Bates.

Paul directed *Lucky's* bow toward the mooring, which Derek snagged with the boathook, inhaling the cool air's clean pine-salt scent as he tied her on.

"Nice place you got here." He and Paul were the only ones on the boat. Most of the wedding guests had already arrived, but Derek hadn't been able to get a flight out of Hawaii until after his last charter ended yesterday. Or was it the day before? God he was tired. But he wouldn't miss Paul's wedding for anything.

"Yeah, it works for us." Paul grinned and slapped him on the back. He had one of those eternally youthful faces, round cheeks, sandy hair and bright blue eyes. At twenty-nine he didn't look a day older than when Derek found him ten years earlier vomiting up too much summertime fun, lost and disoriented in a not-great part of Miami. Derek lived there at the time, working jobs on whatever boats he could, in the years before he got serious about his maritime career and enrolled at the Massachusetts Maritime Academy. Since Paul had had no idea where his friend Kevin lived, Derek let him crash on his floor in the tiny apartment he'd sublet when he wasn't at sea. Didn't take him long to figure out Paul was a good kid caught in a bad situation—a delayed adolescent rebellion against real and imagined pressures of adulthood.

Derek got Paul a job on a boat for the summer, helped him get off booze and back on track to finish college at Notre Dame. In the ensuing years their friendship surpassed big-brother mentor and younger screw-up, and became close and satisfying. About as close and satisfying as any relationship Derek could have these days.

He helped Paul load last-minute supplies into the on-board dinghy and lower the boat into the smooth water.

"You won't know a whole lot of people." Paul climbed into the dinghy and manned the oars. "Sarah, of course."

Of course. Derek settled himself in the bow seat. He'd emailed Paul's sister before coming, hoping she'd put aside her grudge against him, but Sarah was a passionate woman prone to the dramatic, and apparently hadn't forgiven him for thinking it was an extremely bad idea for them to sleep together. Her reply had been coldly formal, but at least she'd replied. "How is Sarah?"

"She's Sarah." Paul spoke of his twin with exasperated affection. "Two parts fabulous, two parts crazy-making. She has her best friend Joe here, and her friend from grade school Addie Sewell."

"Addie." Derek frowned, trying to get his tired brain to function. "That's a familiar name, have I met her?"

"Nope." Paul corrected his course with a few strokes of his right oar. "Grade school friend of ours. I was crazy about her for years."

"Oh, right, the woman who walked on water." Derek had been curious about her. Paul was easygoing about pretty much everything—once he stopped drinking—but this Addie had him in knots. As far as Derek knew, Paul had never let on to Addie how he felt.

"Yeah, I had it bad." Paul shook his head, laughing. "Ellen finally exorcized her completely. Addie's a great friend now."

"Okay. Sarah, Addie. Who else?" The boat nudged onto the generous expanse of sand exposed at half tide. Derek jumped out and grabbed the bowline, pulled the dinghy up onto the beach. At high tide, there was barely enough beach to walk on. At low, twelve vertical feet out, there was ample sand, then ample mud, sprinkled with rocks and starfish, clusters of mussels, and a hidden bounty of steamer clams.

"Some friends from college and a few from work in Boston. Nice people. Oh, and Kevin Ames, who can't make it until tomorrow. I think you met him once." He gave Derek a sheepish look and started unloading the skiff onto a waiting wheelbarrow. "Maybe not under the best circumstances."

"Right." Kevin had been the friend buying Paul booze in Florida in spite of his obvious issues with alcohol, and encouraging him to drop out of college and "find himself." He'd reminded Derek of his own brothers: wealthy, self-centered and entitled, sure rules were for other people and that they'd automatically rise to the top—like most scum. If it wasn't for the sea, which had started calling to Derek in middle school and soon after took him away from the life his parents planned for him, he'd probably be that way himself.

Years of hard work clawing up the ranks from deckhand to captain was enough to beat the entitled out of anybody.

They finished loading the wheelbarrow, secured the dinghy against the rising tide and made their way through the Christmas-tree smelling woods, then up a wide bumpy path through blueberry bushes to the back door of the house, a rambling two-story Victorian with weathered gray shingles and dark green trim and shutters. Pitched in nearby clearings were several colorful tents, obviously for overflow guests, though the house had six or seven bedrooms from what he remembered.

"Hey! Hurry up. Ellen needs the cheese you bought for nachos." Sarah jumped down from the house's back deck and strode to meet them, followed by a tall, dark-haired guy in jeans and a Green Day T-shirt. "Hi, Derek."

"Hey, Sarah." He smiled, relieved when she managed a chilly grin back. Apparently she'd be on good behavior for her brother's wedding. "It's good to see you. You look great."

He wasn't lying. She'd dropped the few extra pounds she'd carried, had shortened and shaped her curly blond hair, and moved with more mature grace, though she still evoked a tall firecracker about to go off.

"Thanks. You look…" She scowled at him. "Like you haven't slept in years."

"Not sure I have. Hi, I'm Derek." He offered his hand to the guy hovering behind her, noting the wary look in his eyes. Was this Joe? Looked like Sarah had shared her I'm-the-victim version of their story with him.

"This is Joe." Sarah pointed.

"Good to meet you." Joe shook Derek's hand then picked up a grocery bag under each arm. "I'll take these up to Ellen."

"Come on in. We're having drinks, getting organized to take a picnic supper down to the beach." Sarah turned and charged back up the stairs to the house, throwing Derek an inscrutable look over her shoulder that made him a little nervous. He'd had to put her off gently on that same beach five years ago, and he really didn't want to go through that drama again.

The pine and faint wood smoke smell inside the house was instantly familiar. Paul's parents were on the mainland, so instead of Mrs. Bosson at the stove, there was a blonde, attractive woman Derek identified as Ellen by the adoring look she sent Paul, and whom he instantly liked by the bright smile she sent him. The aroma in the kitchen was fantastic.

"Welcome, Derek." She gave him a sincere hug, Southern accent warming her words. Paul had met her through a mutual friend in Boston two years earlier and his fate was sealed pretty quickly. "It's good to meet the man who saved Paul's life."

"I don't think it was quite that dramatic."

"I know it was. He's still grateful and so am I." A timer went off; she grabbed lobster oven mitts and peered into the oven.

Derek looked around the large, airy eat-in kitchen, amused and pleased so much of it was exactly the same as the last time he was here. The loon sculpture, the blobby painting of a seal Sarah had done as a girl, sand dollars and sea glass, a tide clock hanging next to an iron candle holder forged by a local blacksmith. He'd only been here a week, but would never forget the strong sense of love surrounding the Bosson family, and their joy at being together. He hadn't had much of that in his life, still didn't, and he'd unapologetically eaten it up. Paul had invited him back a few times, but their schedules never seemed to mesh.

"Can I help, Ellen?"

"No, no." She set a pan of fragrant rolls onto a cooling rack. "I just got rid of my army of helpers and am finishing in here. Grab a beer and go on outside, I'll join you in a minute."

"Here you go." Paul pulled bottles of beer and lemonade from the old gas refrigerator and tossed the beer to Derek, who was afraid drinking would send him into a coma of exhaustion, but hell, it was a celebration. He'd risk it.

He followed Paul outside, where Paul was immediately pounced on and dragged into conversation. Derek paused on the front stoop, newly entranced by the Bossons' view. The house sat high on a hill. The land in front—you couldn't really call it a yard—was covered by juniper bushes and sloped to a steep cliff with a breathtaking panorama of ocean and islands. More tents were pitched to the west of the house, and a tiny cabin, built for the twins to overnight in, perched to the east. At this hour the sun's full strength had started to wane and colors were deepening—the blue of water, the dark green of firs, gray-brown shades of the rocky coastline, and the puffy white of clouds. One of his favorite places on earth. And given that he'd been all over the world and was working out of Hawaii these days, he had plenty of Edens to choose from.

Taking a deep breath of the cool, salty air, he shifted his focus to the other guests, in groups on the front porch and down on the grounds. Fifteen to twenty people. At thirty-five, he probably had five to ten years on most of them. It had been a long time since he'd been in this type of social situation. On his boat, he was the authority, keeping just enough distance from guests and employees, making the ship's safety and smooth operation his first priority, the comfort of his passengers a close second. Onshore, he was a temporary or occasional friend to whomever he knew or met wherever he was.

He took a bigger slug of beer than he needed. Paul caught his eye and raised a finger, indicating he'd be right back. Derek waved him off and took another drink. He was a grown man; he could introduce himself to—

"Hi." The woman was right under his nose, smiling at him, about to come up the steps as he'd been about to go down.

"I'm Addie." She pointed to her chest, as if he might not know for sure she was talking about herself.

So this was Addie. To put it mildly, she was not what he expected.

The way Paul had described her beauty, wealth, breeding and untouchability in his besotted way had Derek imagining a chilly, elegant brunette dripping sophistication and disdain. The kind who'd show up at a casual island wedding like this one in stiletto heels, linen and pearls. The kind Derek had taken around the world in his boat, the kind with rich older husbands they were always looking to cheat on.

This woman was wearing soft-looking midthigh black shorts, a casual rose-colored scoop-necked top half covered by a gray hoodie, and flat natural color sandals on slim feet. She had deep coffee eyes and striking dark brows, curling short dark hair—a sexy-schoolgirl fantasy come to life. She reminded him of a down-to-earth version of the French actress Audrey Tautou.

He had major hots for Audrey Tautou.

"You're Addie Sewell."

"Yes." The expressive brows lowered in amused confusion. "How did you know?"

"You're world famous."

"Ha!" Her wide mouth broke into a smile that took away a good deal of his weariness. "You must be a friend of Paul's."

"Derek Bates."

"Oh." Her smile faltered, her eyes clouded over, the temperature around them dropped forty degrees. Brrrrr. "Sarah's told me a lot about you."

"That's funny." He forced himself to chuckle, visualizing a roll of duct tape over Sarah's mouth. "Sarah doesn't know a lot about me."

He expected an insult, an argument, a stinging defense of her friend, and was surprised to find her considering him thoughtfully. "I just know what she told me."

Derek sighed. He'd leave bad enough alone. It was his word versus Sarah's and this was her territory and these were her people. "I'm pretty sure I'm sorry to hear that. When did you arrive, Addie?"

"Three days ago. Sunday evening."

"From…?"

"LaGuardia." She glanced around, apparently not sure she should be talking to him.

"Into Portland?"

"Bangor."

"Okay." He nodded too many times, at a loss what to say next, how to act around a lovely woman who'd undoubtedly been told by her best friend that he was something you should avoid stepping in.

"Weather been good here this week?" *Really, Derek? The weather?*

"It's been okay." She fidgeted with the zipper on her hoodie. "Not great. But at least no rain."

"What have I missed so far?"

"Oh. Well. We've gone hiking on the mainland. Done a lot of hanging out…" She laughed nervously. "I can't really remember."

"It's okay."

"Oh, Quoddy Head. We went there. The easternmost point in the U.S."

"Nice." He nodded again. This was torture. He wanted to skip the small talk. Go straight to what mattered, how she felt about life, whether she was doing what she loved, whether the world was a gorgeous place or a disaster, whether she was seeing anyone, and whether she liked kissing all night under the stars…

He nearly hugged Ellen when she clapped her hands from the front stoop.

"Hey, y'all, we're ready. Come through the kitchen, grab something to carry and we'll head down to the beach."

Derek finished his beer and tossed it into the recycling container set up outside. If he wanted to have fun this week he'd need to do better than this socially. Part of his job was chatting with passengers, so making small talk should be second nature. Instead he felt as if he were trying to exercise a muscle atrophied from years of disuse.

After grabbing a cooler, he joined the procession to the beach, aware of Addie's presence in the crowd as if she was lit up in neon. He still couldn't get over how different she was than he expected, or how much she aroused his…curiosity.

The beach was cool and comfortable; a light breeze kept the mosquitoes manageable, though repellent was passed around before everyone settled in. To his relief, Derek eventually got a second—third? fourth?—wind, and was able to relax and enjoy himself. The guests were friendly and easy to talk to, all interesting people with solid views on life and their places in it. The food was simple and abundant: excellent crab rolls, nachos, potato salad and coleslaw, and the beer flowed like…beer.

A few times—more than a few—he glanced over at Addie and caught her just looking away, though she made no move to approach him. He wasn't sure what to make of her surreptitious inspection. Was she repulsed? Fascinated? Attracted? He was certainly attracted. The more he looked at her, the longer the evening went on, the more he remembered stories Paul told about Addie, the more he was intrigued, and the more beautiful she became. Maybe it was the softening light. Maybe it was the beer. He wanted to talk to her again. Alone.

As the sun lowered, there was a move to light a bonfire and gather around it. Not enough sleep and too much beer, food and conversation propelled Derek to his feet. He could use a break and had a deep need to watch the sunset from a remote corner of the island he remembered as a prime viewing spot. A quick look showed him Addie was missing from the crowd. He'd have liked to invite her along, but that was probably a terrible idea given what she still thought of him, so it was just as well.

Excusing himself from Sarah's friend Joe, who'd turned out to be an interesting and friendly guy, and Carrie, a piece of work who'd settled on Joe after flirting with pretty much every male at the party, Derek left the beach and headed back into the woods up the hill toward the southwest where he could best watch the evening light show.

As he crested the hill, he glanced back at the house; its shingles glowed majestic gray-pink in the evening light, tents providing a festive carnival atmosphere.

Addie Sewell was coming down the front steps.

Derek stopped short. When she caught sight of him, she did the same. For a few bizarre seconds they stared at each other across the grassy space, then what-the-hell, Derek beckoned to her. She frowned and looked down toward the path to the beach.

This might take some persuading.

"Hey." He spanned the distance between them across the top of the hill, brushing past goldenrod waving in the breeze. Addie held her ground, chin lifted, watching him approach. "I'm going to take a walk, to check out the sunset."

She pressed her lips together. An adorable dimple appeared in her right cheek. "Sounds like a good idea."

"Want to come with me?"

"Oh." She blushed crimson, eyes darting again to the apparent safety of the woods. Poor woman, trapped by the big bad sexual predator Derek wasn't. "I don't know…."

He'd wait. He swatted a mosquito. Stuffed his hands in his pockets and rocked back and forth on his heels. Began whistling.

She giggled. A good sign.

"The sunsets here are breathtaking…."

"Well." She gave him a cautious sidelong look. "It has been either cloudy or foggy since I've been here."

He grinned. "I'll keep my clothes on and my hands to myself, I promise."

"Oh, no, you don't need to—" Her eyes shot wide. "Wait! No, yes, you do!"

He laughed and she laughed with him, and then bang, the tension was gone, and he felt lighter than he had all day.

"What I meant was, I'm not worried." She arched a brow at him. "I have a spectacular right hook, three gold medals in track and a black belt."

"Weaponry?"

She pointed emphatically into his face. "That, too."

"I'll remember." He smiled, trying to look as blandly safe as possible, so she wouldn't guess the depth of his attraction. After what she'd probably heard from Sarah, he should act like touching her had never occurred to him.

Though it was starting to be all he could think about.

"So you must have been on Storness Island before, Addie?" He gestured her onto the narrow path in front of him, being the perfect gentleman. The perfect gentleman who wasn't wrong in thinking her rear view would not exactly be a hardship.

"Actually, no. Sarah invited me a few times, but my parents always had me in summer camp or some program, or we were traveling. So this is new to me."

"Sounds like you were a heavily scheduled kid."

"Oh, yeah. They played Mozart while I was in utero. I got infant flash cards, only educational toys, organic food before it was mainstream, you name it." She spoke matter-of-factly. Was she grateful? Resentful? Resigned? He wanted to get at more of her, only barely understanding his fascination.

"How was that?"

She shrugged, keeping her eyes on the path, an obstacle course of rocks and protruding tree roots. "It was all I knew, so it was fine at the time. Now, it seems a little over the top. They'd lightened up some by the time my brother came along. He's five years younger. What about you?"

"I'm the oldest of four brothers. My parents did the overachiever conditioning on us, too. It worked pretty well on my brothers. I wasn't interested." He reached to touch her shoulder and pointed into the bay where the sunset was gathering force. "Look at that."

"Beautiful." She stopped walking, then smiled rapturously and stretched out her arms, as if wanting to embrace the bay. "Don't you wish all of life was that simple and perfect? After living in the city so long it's like…well, I miss things like this at home."

He knew how she felt. "What city? Wait, near LaGuardia obviously, so I'll guess New York?"

"Manhattan. Where's home for you?"

He quirked an eyebrow. "That's a tough question to answer. I don't have one in the traditional sense."

"Oh, right." She turned and kept walking. "You're the yacht captain."

He expected the slight sneer. Most people had no idea what the job entailed, how serious his responsibilities and how wide his range of duties. "I'm based in Hawaii right now."

"Ooh, *that* must be tough."

He caught up to her as the path widened down a cranberry-covered hillside, red berries a stunning contrast to the carpet of dark, shiny leaves. "It has its moments. What do you do in Manhattan?"

"I'm an actuary for an insurance company."

"Ah, a numbers woman." And a very smart woman.

He was impressed. Maybe she'd like to take over for his bookkeeper, Mary, who was due to go on maternity leave in another month. "How do you cope with Manhattan being Manhattan?"

Her mouth puckered a little while she thought. The sun landed on her cheekbones and lit her eyes. He was hit with a strong urge to kiss her. But since he'd only just met her and was trying to show how wrong Sarah was about him...not a good idea.

"In Manhattan you have to retreat into your head. You can't go out there every day and let the chaos get in your face. At least I can't. It's strange what you get used to. A friend on the phone the other day said she could barely understand me over sirens in the background and I hadn't even heard them."

"Noisy, crowded, sounds perfect."

"Oh, but there's so much culture. So much energy. Anything you want to eat, buy, hear or see, you can find in New York." She smiled mischievously, mouth generous, lips full. "How do you deal with all that total isolation in the middle of the ocean?"

"Ha. Good question. My answer would probably be something along the lines of, 'I retreat into my head. You can't go out there and let the emptiness get in your face.'" He loved the way she laughed, soft and low. "And of course there's so much beauty. So much peace."

"Speaking of which..." They'd arrived on the rocky ledge he remembered as the best spot for sunset watching. He wasn't wrong. The sight was spectacular. Addie crossed her arms; her breasts rose and nestled against each other. She sighed in pleasure.

Derek swallowed. Lack of sleep, beer, this woman...

He was beginning to understand what had happened to Paul.

"I'm curious." She turned to face him, eyes doe-wide and questioning. The gods were putting his resolve not to touch her to an excruciating test. He wasn't sure he'd pass. "Did you always want to be at sea instead of settled in one place?"

"Yes. Did you always want to be in the same office and house every day?

"Not specifically, no. But it didn't surprise me I ended up there." She tipped her head, mouth spreading again, this time in a troubled smile that was both vulnerable and bewitching.

Derek should step back from her. Derek should stop thinking about her and start thinking about tragedies or trash heaps or tarantulas. Derek needed a good night's sleep. Or twelve. "Why not?"

"I didn't have a childhood dream like yours. I always did what was expected of me. My parents prepared me well for my future, and I felt I owed it to them to be successful."

Ah, a good girl. She was really turning him on now. He wanted to teach her how to be naughty sometimes. "There are all kinds of success."

"True." She brushed a stray lock off her forehead. "I guess I'm pretty traditional. Not that exciting."

Ha. He wasn't touching that one. Instead he turned her and pointed out into the bay. "Look now."

"Oh." Her face brightened; it was all he could do to make himself watch the sunset he was here for. "Incredible."

"Yes. Beautiful." She could think he was talking about the glorious colors if she wanted. The sun was slipping through a vivid combination of orange and maroon at the horizon. Higher up the clouds had turned baby-girl pink. Seagulls flew overhead; cormorants skimmed the water, heading toward the navy-colored east. The moment was powerful, primal. Addie had him under a spell he barely understood.

He moved up close behind her until he could practically feel the warmth from her body. She tensed and went very still.

"Addie." His voice came out low and husky. She made a small sound, but didn't answer. He barely knew what he was going to say. "Did you...ever meet a guy and know you'd be kissing him very soon?"

She flinched, but didn't move away. "Derek...I don't even know you."

"I'm just asking." Like hell he was.

"Oh. Well. Yes. I mean...I guess so." She cleared her throat. "Have you?"

"I'm not really into kissing guys."

A nervous giggle exploded out of her. "I meant—"

"I know what you meant. Yes, I have."

"Oh." She sounded carefully neutral. "Why did you ask me that?"

"I wanted to know."

Addie turned her head to the side, her features darkened by the light behind her. "What happened between you and Sarah?"

"She obviously told you."

"I want to hear it from you."

He was absurdly pleased. She was giving him a chance. But since she was already on Sarah's side, he'd have to choose his words carefully. "Sarah and I...mixed signals one night. When things didn't work out the way she expected she was angry and hurt. She's a great person, I respect her and would go back and change that night if I could."

Addie turned around to look up at him, stopping mere

inches away. God help him. "She told me you came on to her."

"No." He held still while she examined his face, wanting to touch her so badly he was having trouble breathing, aware that he'd just called her close friend a liar.

"Did you ask me about kissing because you wanted to kiss me?"

"What do you think?"

He expected a giggle. A blush. A coy glance. Instead she looked distraught. "Derek, I'm...I'm here to be with someone."

A solid kick to his stomach. "Yeah? Who's that?"

She dropped her gaze. "Someone I've known a long time."

He would have noticed if she'd been hanging around any guy in particular tonight. As far as he knew all the guests had arrived.

Except...*him.*

Aw, crap. "Kevin Ames."

"How did you know?" She was blushing.

"He's world famous." He kept his voice light, not wanting to sound as disappointed and pissed off as he was. "I've met him."

"Really?" Her voice got all eager, which made Derek even grouchier. "Where?"

"In Florida." He was not going to comment further. If Kevin was the type she fell for, she wasn't going to want a man like him.

He shouldn't care. For God's sake, he'd only met Addie tonight.

Maybe it was the booze, the loss of sleep, too much loneliness for too long, but there were plenty of attractive women here, many of whom he'd spoken to at dinner—

hell there had been plenty of attractive women crawling all over his boat for the last eight years.

It was crazy, it made no sense, he was exhausted, out of his mind, he'd known Addie all of a few hours.

But he'd never wanted any of them the way he wanted her.

3

SARAH LAY ON a grassy patch at the edge of the island's northern beach, where they'd had dinner that evening, listening to the waves lapping, gazing up at the night sky in search of shooting stars. She'd gone inside with everyone else hours ago when the party broke up, but after people headed off to bed she'd come back out here, knowing she wouldn't sleep. Too many emotions, her head spun with them. She hated feeling half-crazy like this.

For whatever reason she'd been born feeling things more intensely than most people, which earned her all kinds of lovely labels: diva, drama queen, yeah, yeah, she knew. She did overreact, she did get more upset, more happy, more…just more. But short of drugging herself, there was nothing she could do about it. She was who she was, for better or worse.

Right now worse.

She swallowed awkwardly over the mild burn of thirst in the back of her throat. One beer too many and not enough water to balance out the alcohol. But it was so lovely lying here watching the sky, indulging her tortured thoughts, that she didn't want to go back up to the house for a drink.

Derek Bates was the most gorgeous, sexiest, most intelligent, incredible man she'd ever met. And Sarah was nothing to him. She always fell for men who didn't want her. Before Derek there'd been Ethan at Vassar, captain of the baseball team, a great friend. She'd lusted, but he never thought of her "that way" and had dated cheerleaders and dancers and other varieties of perfect—from her perspective perfectly vapid—women, while maintaining a closer relationship with Sarah than with any of them. Before Ethan there'd been Kevin Ames. She'd had it bad for Kevin for a long, long time. But when he finally stopped chasing big-boobed wonders, he'd wanted Addie, not Sarah. Maybe he still did…that would be great, actually. If Sarah couldn't have him, at least one of her best friends could; for Addie's sake Sarah would do whatever it took to bring them together this week. Addie needed someone. She had no idea how fabulous she was.

But back to Sarah's favorite topic: Sarah. What if she never got Derek out of her head or her heart, even knowing he'd never belong to her?

That night five years ago on this beach, she'd been a total brat, which she was still so horribly embarrassed about she could barely look at him.

Although seriously, who could not look at Derek? She still did, just not when he could tell.

Anyway, it had been a cool and moonless night, like this one. They'd sat on this very spot talking for an hour after Paul and their parents had gone to bed. Sarah had been drunk on too much wine and had started bawling over something, she couldn't even remember what. Derek had comforted her, put his arms around her, stroked her hair. She'd thought that was the signal she'd been dreaming of and had tried her best to make something happen.

Yeah, well, nice fantasy, Sarah.

Then, in an appalling show of immaturity, she'd bolstered her crushed ego by accusing him to Addie and then to Joe, who when she came back to Vassar had been able to tell right away that something was upsetting her. It didn't help that she'd also overheard comments from Paul about Derek's sexploits in harbors around the world. A woman in every port, sometimes two, and in St. Thomas, three, two of whom were apparently twins. So even not caring much who he had in bed at any given time, he still hadn't wanted Sarah.

She coughed. Man, she needed water. Her throat was practically sticking to itself.

Footsteps rustled and snapped in the woods. Sarah lifted onto her elbows. A man's form, stepping onto the beach, well-built, tall. Her heart starting to race. Derek? Coming to finish what they started?

"Sarah?"

Joe. Her heart slowed. She sat up. "Yes, it's me."

"What are you doing out here?"

"Couldn't sleep. How did you know where I was?"

"I heard you leave, didn't hear you come back so I came looking." He plunked down on the grass beside her and handed her something cool.

A can of sparkling water. "Joe, you are a god."

"Wait, you're only realizing that now?"

"No, no, I knew." She cracked the top to the can and took a long, grateful drink. "Heaven. Thank you."

"You're welcome. So what are you doing out here besides not sleeping?"

"Watching for shooting stars. Thinking."

"About what?" He scooched down to lie next to her. His warm side adjacent to her hip made her realize she'd gotten chilly.

"About…how I always fall for guys who don't want me."

"No kidding. You're batting about a thousand on that one."

"Ha." Sarah giggled. "Thanks for the vote of support."

"I mean how can anyone be so clueless?"

"Hey." She shoved him with her hip. "Your deep empathy is much appreciated."

"You can't see what's right under your nose, Sarah Bosson." His voice descended to a melodramatic growl.

"Okay, okay. So what do I do?"

"Come to Dr. Joe. He will rewire your brain using everyday household items."

Sarah's laughter was interrupted by a horrific burp from the soda bubbles. She laughed harder. "Oh, no! Joe, I'm so sorry."

"It's fine, don't worry, really. I still have hearing in my other ear."

"Stop, stop." She waited for her giggles to die out, loving that she could belch in front of Joe and not feel more than slightly embarrassed. He had no illusions she was perfect. He had no illusions about her at all. And for some reason he still wanted to be her friend.

They'd met at Vassar and became close right away. After graduating they'd both moved to Boston where she got a job fund-raising for Harvard and he did something with computers she couldn't begin to understand. They saw each other a few times a month and talked and texted often. He was her absolute rock. She'd die without him. "Anyway, so I was thinking about this one unattainable guy who—"

"Derek."

Sarah's jaw dropped. That was psychic, even for him.

Or maybe she was pathetically obvious. "How did you know?"

"You mooned over him all night."

"I did not!" Yup. Pathetic.

"Because he's so hunky and sexy and sooo super hot!"

Sarah made a sound of exasperation. "Well, he is."

"I know, I know." Joe's sigh was heavy in the darkness. "Go ahead, Sarah, talk. You know I can take it."

"Well, I have to tell you something." She hunched her shoulders, hugging her knees, hoping he wouldn't be angry. "That night with Derek on the beach."

His body tensed next to her. "Yes?"

"He didn't attack me. I was drunk and I sort of…tried to make something happen."

"I figured it was something like that."

"Wait, what?" She released her knee to whap his shoulder. "How dare you undermine the power of my dramatic bombshell?"

"Aw, Sarah." He reached up to push her bangs off her face, let his fingers drift tenderly down her cheek. "I've known you for nine years. If you were really attacked by some guy, he wouldn't live long enough to see the next day, let alone the next five years. The way Paul talks about this guy, the way you talk about him, it didn't add up. I didn't know exactly what happened, but I'm not surprised."

She lay down next to him, throat tight. "You don't blame me?"

"For what?"

"Lying?"

"I didn't think of it that way. You just weren't ready to tell the whole truth."

Her heart was full to bursting. She had to blink through

tears to bring the stars back into focus. "Seriously, Joe, are you perfect or do you just pretend to be?"

"I'm the real deal, Sarah. Maybe someday you'll realize—"

A white streak blazed across a good portion of the night sky. Sarah shrieked and pointed. "Did you see *that?*"

"Whoa. Yes. I did." He sounded as awed as she felt. "It means you get to make a wish."

"Why not you?"

"You saw it first."

"How do you know?"

"Because." He reached over and rubbed her head until her already messy hair was a total disaster, making her shriek again, with laughter this time. "I said so."

"Stop! My coif! My stunning updo. Ruined!"

"Now." He let her go. "Make a wish."

"Okay, okay." Sarah thought—took her about half a second to decide—then reached up to the sky and wished with all her might that she might love a man who loved her back. It was all she'd ever wanted. So many people managed it. Her parents. Paul and Ellen. Why not her?

"Finished?"

"Yes."

"Should I check?"

Sarah frowned. "Check what?"

"To see if the six hottest members of the U.S. Navy are waiting naked in your room?"

She giggled. "That's *not* what I wished for."

"Then I hope you get whatever it was." He got to his feet, reached down and pulled her up opposite him as if she weighed nothing. "And I think you need to go to bed."

"Yes, Dad." She didn't resist when his arms came around her. He was such a good friend. So patient with her, so nonthreatening. Why couldn't she fall in love with him?

"Listen to me."

"Mmm?" She laid her head on his solid shoulder.

"You are going to sleep really well tonight." He started stroking her hair, working the tense muscles at the base of her scalp. "And tomorrow you are going to wake up and realize you've put this Derek demon totally to bed."

"Okay." She closed her eyes. As if. She'd be happy if she could think about him without getting wet. And talk to him without getting so flustered and guilty she could barely form words.

"And." Joe rocked her back and forth. "You are going to remind yourself that I love you no matter how insane you get, no matter how completely and insufferably annoying, no matter how—"

"Uh, Joe?" She patted his chest. "Yeah, um, thanks. That's enough."

"No problem." He squeezed her then took her hand. "Let's go."

"I'm ready." She followed him across the beach, fumbling for her flashlight. "Hey, who was that girl you were talking to all night? The cute little one."

"Carrie?"

"Yeah. Where's your flashlight?" She tried to remember seeing him use one, still not having any luck extracting hers from her sweatshirt pocket since it was on the side of the hand Joe was holding.

"Don't need one. Just follow me."

"Wait, seriously? Through the woods? The path is treacherous and it's pitch-black. I've come here all my life and even I wouldn't do it."

"I have cat eyes."

"Joe…" She hung back, still trying for the flashlight, until he tugged her impatiently forward.

"Just lift your feet so you don't trip. You'll be fine."

"Okay. But if you kill me I'm suing." She followed him a few more steps, getting braver as it became apparent he was navigating nicely. "So…what about Carrie?"

"Nice girl. What do you want to know?"

"I don't know." Her voice came out too high and she had to relax her throat to get it back to normal. "Do you like her?"

He snorted impatiently. "No, I talked to her all night because she repulsed me."

"Okay, okay. Never mind." Sarah's giggle felt forced. What was wrong with her, she was so self-absorbed she couldn't even be happy for her best friend? "I'm glad for you. I hope something comes of it. You deserve someone wonderful."

"I think so, too." He pulled her up unerringly through the trees, finding the path past the blueberry patch and up to the house, supporting her when she stumbled. It was actually kind of mysterious and cool.

"I don't know what I'd do without you, Joe."

He chuckled and opened the back door for her to go inside. "I hope you never have to find out."

She kissed his cheek and crossed through the living room toward the bedroom she shared with Addie, noticing how much calmer and lighter she felt, how much more clear and slow-moving her brain was. Joe was good for her. He always had been. Knew her inside out, tolerated her worst faults and adored her strengths. What more could a woman want?

Macho alpha sizzle. Daring, adventure, challenge.

Sarah sighed and used the hall bathroom, then climbed into bed, careful not to disturb Addie.

Sometimes she thought she must be the most shallow person alive. But if she was deep-down wired to be attracted to guys like Derek, Ethan and Kevin instead of guys like Joe, there wasn't a single damn thing she could do about it.

4

ADDIE WAS CONFUSED. Standing on the cliff in front of the Bossons' house, drinking champagne punch, keeping an eye out for Kevin's arrival, she was in a thorough state of turmoil. And since confusion didn't visit her very often, thank goodness, she could safely say that she didn't like it. At all. Most of the time her emotional life was, if not under control, then at least comprehensible. She was single or she was in a relationship. She was friends with someone or she wasn't. She had a crush on a guy or she didn't.

She'd come to this island with a head full of Kevin. Her past with him, the promise of intimate time with him this weekend, and the vaguest whisper of possibility that they could continue some relationship into the future—Philadelphia wasn't that far from New York City after all. Over a decade of mooning and fantasy about to come true.

And then she met Derek.

Her love of the simple and the clear—statistics and probabilities and interpretable data—did not prepare her for a man who, during their first-ever meeting unsettled her to the point of blathering, who wanted to watch the sunset alone with her, and who, in a low, dreamy voice, as much as said he wanted to kiss her. Frankly, for a few seconds—okay, many seconds—she'd wanted him to kiss her more than she'd wanted to go on breathing.

Even if Sarah's story about Derek wasn't one-hundred percent accurate, as Derek claimed, he was still a girl-in-every-port guy in his mid-thirties, while Kevin, at thirty-one, had already been totally committed to one woman in a marriage, faithful until divorce did them part.

Shouldn't that clear everything up? A rational conclusion drawn from the available information, leading to a sensible low-risk recommendation for future action. Derek was a womanizer. Kevin was a sweetheart. Only an idiot would still dream about Derek. Or do something completely foolish like keep peeking over at him on a kayak trip earlier that afternoon. She'd interrupted perfectly wonderful chances to stare into the water, spot orange and purple starfish, waving seaweed that looked nearly floral, blue mussels and splotchy pink growths on underwater reefs by looking up every three seconds to keep track of where he was and with whom. Worse, she'd caught him several times in the act of looking over at her, too.

For a while he'd paddled alongside her kayak, and they'd chatted easily about his extensive travels and her not-so-extensive ones. About movies and books and favorite foods. Through it all, he'd shown no signs of anything more than friendly interest, and then he'd quite naturally steered his kayak over to chat with someone else.

Well, of course, right? He was here to get to know Paul's friends, too. Plus the guy had put himself out there with her last night and she'd stomped him flat, why *would* he continue to show interest?

And why couldn't she stop wanting him to?

Greedy Addie, wanting her hunk and to eat him, too.

She giggled at her own thought and nearly spit out the sip of punch she'd just taken. The group was assembled after quick-as-possible showers to save the water supply, enjoying a predinner drink or two.

The group minus Paul. Paul was not on the island because Paul had gone to the mainland to pick up *Kevin*.

Eek!

Addie was as light as the champagne, as bubbly as the…champagne, as fizzy as the…um, well…champagne. And clearly not big on similes.

Paul had been gone over an hour, which meant any minute he'd be back. Addie had come down by the cliff here, hoping to catch the first glance of *Lucky's* approach, so she would know exactly when to start freaking out.

Or she could get a head start and do it *now*.

Closing her eyes, she inhaled deeply, fighting a sudden deep desire to be home organizing Great-Aunt Grace's papers. So easy. So uncomplicated. This paper goes in this pile. That goes in that one.

"Hello, Addie."

She started at the sound of Derek's voice, luckily not standing close enough to the edge to pitch over. She immediately had to put the brakes on a fantasy of Derek saving her from certain death by hauling her back into his arms.

Honestly. Addie pulled herself together. "Hey, there, Derek."

Then she made a fatal error. She turned to look at him.

He was breathtaking. A touch more sun on his cheeks made the contrast even sexier between golden skin and his white shirt, and made his vivid eyes practically jump out of his face.

No, no, *Kevin* was coming soon. Once glance at him and everything she'd ever felt for him over so many years would come rushing back again, and this Derek guy would be forgotten.

"Enjoying the view?"

"I am." She put on a casual smile—ho-hum, nice to see you—and concentrated on the view, which she'd just been pretending to look at before. Yes, it was lovely. A sailboat was cruising in toward the bay, sails crisp white in the sunshine. A lobsterman was hauling traps just beyond the next island, his white and green boat bobbing gently in the waves. Breezes ruffled her hair; the air was sweet enough to drink. Why hadn't she been enjoying this all along? "I don't think I'd ever get tired of this view. The sea is always changing, the light, the birds, the boats…"

Derek chuckled. "Well, Ms. Manhattan. You're describing the view I see pretty much every day. Maybe you need to give that life a try."

She snorted, having to suppress yet another picture, this one of herself sunbathing on the deck of his yacht. "Do they pay full-time salary and benefits for someone to project the odds of running aground or sinking?"

"Um…" He tapped a finger on his very sexy lips as if trying to remember. "Not really, no. But I have an on-board bookkeeping position opening up in a few weeks. Are you interested?"

"Don't think so, but thanks." Addie made another serious mistake. She smiled at him. Then he smiled at her, and it was as if the scene around them wrapped itself up neatly and disappeared, the way backgrounds did sometimes in cartoons, leaving the two of them alone in nothingness.

Worse than how she'd felt the night before when she'd had to force herself to watch one of the most magnificent sunsets she'd ever seen. All she'd wanted to do was gaze into those cinnamon-brown eyes and drool.

Okay, Addie. Engage rational superpowers immediately. Like this: fine to look, fine to appreciate, but no touching.

An upswell of voices by the house made her turn to see what was happening.

Kevin was happening. Somehow she'd missed being first to see the boat, hadn't heard it, either, and now he was right here, standing on the front porch, being hugged by Ellen, two or three others crowding around for their turns, grinning that old familiar straight-toothed grin that could still knock her for a loop.

And just like that, as if she'd been released from a sorcerer's spell, Addie was able to move again, to walk away from the awesome but evil power that was Derek, and into the pure heavenly light of Kevin.

"Ad-*die*." The last syllable of her name came out on a shout. She'd forgotten the special way he said it, and the memory made her legs move even faster. And there he was, disentangling himself from the other woman and sailing down the steps on his strong runner's legs to grab and whirl her around in a joyous embrace that made her laugh and gasp for breath and nearly spill her punch.

Kevin Ames.

"God, look at you." He held her at arm's length, his face glowing. Eleven years later, he looked exactly the same. Maybe his face was thinner, maybe his skin was a bit weathered, and now that she looked, had he lightened his hair? But really, exactly the same. "You've turned into one seriously hot babe, Addie!"

His face might be glowing, hers was on fire. "Thanks, Kevin. You really—"

"Addie all grown up." He shook his head, looking her closely up and down. Somewhat disturbingly, she noticed his eyes were the exact shade of brown as Derek's. Medium caramel. Only for some reason they weren't doing quite the same things to her. "Addie Sewell. I can't believe it. You're a real woman now."

"Oh, well." She was taken aback by his seductive tone then chided herself for being such a prude. Kevin wanting her was the whole point. "I just did the normal grow—"

"What were you, seventeen, eighteen last time I saw you?"

She nodded, unable to blush any harder than she was, or she'd try. "Eighteen."

"I remember that time very well, Addie." His voice lowered, his gaze turned tender. He touched her under the chin, making her shiver. "We never quite got synced up, you and me."

"Uh, no. Not quite." She peeked up at him under her lashes, trying not to be mortified by the memory of her outburst at their last meeting. He certainly didn't seem to hold it against her. "I was a little naive."

"You *were?*" One eyebrow rose suggestively. "So that means you're not anymore?"

Man, her blush mechanism was going to wear out at this rate. But this was what she had come for. No matter how loudly Aunt Grace's boxes were calling to her, no matter how uneasy and rattled she felt around Kevin, she wasn't going to be the shy hide-away girl anymore. "No, Kevin. Not anymore."

"I'm really glad to hear that, Addie." He leaned in close, caught and intertwined her fingers with his, gave them a squeeze. "I've always had a soft spot for you. Actually... sometimes a *hard* spot."

She caught herself just before she cringed, and smiled up at him without shame this time, waiting for the world to disappear around them the way it had around her and Derek.

Waiting...

And...

Hmm.

Well, she felt all warm and melty and sweet, that was something, right?

Plenty.

"Kevin!" A guy Addie barely knew—John, she thought—one of Paul and Kevin's old track buddies charged out of the house and Kevin bolted away for the chest-bumping man-hug.

Addie grinned at the macho ritual then on impulse turned around, feeling eyes burning into her back.

He was still there, feet planted apart, hands on his hips, looking grimmer than she'd ever seen him, or pretty much anyone, look.

Not because of her and Kevin?

No. He didn't look sulky or immature or sour-grapes. He looked…angry. And strong. And nobly determined.

And sexy as hell.

Turning head away, lalala, can't seeeee you!

"Addie." Sarah bounded toward her, drink in hand. "We have *got* to talk."

"Now?" She peered around Sarah at Kevin, relieved to have an excuse not to look back at Derek again. "Can't I have a few more minutes?"

"No." Sarah grabbed her hand and pulled her away from the crowd, across the top of the hill where Addie and Derek had walked the night before.

"What is it, Sarah?"

"I have to tell you something."

"I figured that much." She was used to Sarah's drama, but this time Sarah seemed uncharacteristically uneasy. Usually Addie had the feeling that underneath the wailing and gnashing of teeth, Sarah was enjoying herself immensely. Not this time. "What's going on, are you okay?"

"Fine. Better than ever. But I should have told you this

before. Years ago. Coming here made it really clear." She took a deep breath. "It's about Derek."

"Yes?" Addie had a feeling she knew what was coming. If Sarah's story matched the one Derek told, that meant he'd been telling the truth.

"That night with Derek and me. He wasn't— I was the one—" She gripped Addie's arm, blue eyes wide and earnest, then seemed unable to go on.

"You made the move on him."

"Yes." Breath exploded out of her, Sarah-size relief. "Yes."

"It's okay, Sarah."

"I'm so sorry I—" She frowned. "Hey, how did you know?"

Addie took a leisurely sip of punch, deciding how to answer. She could tell Sarah that Derek let it slip, but wasn't sure it was her place to frame him. And she'd definitely had her own doubts about Sarah's story. "Your anger at him was a little over the top. I wasn't sure, but I thought something didn't feel right."

"Jeez, you, too?"

"Who else?"

"Joe. He said he figured it out pretty much right away." She looked suddenly troubled. "That girl Carrie is really after him, have you noticed."

Addie studied her friend closely. Was she jealous? Addie could only hope. Joe had been deeply in love with her for so long. It was heartbreaking to watch. Sarah had to realize on some level how perfect they were together. He calmed her down and adored her; she spruced him up and gave him purpose. But who knew if she'd ever let herself admit it. "Can you blame her?"

"No, of course not." She laughed too carelessly. "Joe is the perfect man. I tell him so all the time."

"Exactly." Addie smirked, enjoying the situation. Sarah was jealous! Addie would be so pleased if Joe got his happy ever after with her. "Maybe they'll end up together."

"Maybe." She bit her lower lip. "I'm not sure she's his type, though. She's too...obvious."

"Uh-huh. Yeah, men hate when women make them feel totally sexy and desired."

Sarah glared at her. "Not helping."

"Trust me, he won't even notice her extreme beauty and large breasts and—"

"So you're not angry about Derek?" The abrupt subject change nearly made Addie laugh, but out of pity she switched gears, wondering if Carrie might be the answer to Joe's prayers in a way Sarah didn't even suspect.

"No, I'm not angry. He hurt you, and you lashed out, and then felt trapped by the lie. Welcome to the human race."

"Aww, thank you, sweetie. I'm not sure I deserve forgiveness." Sarah gave Addie a fierce hug. "But now wait, we need to talk about the most important thing. How are you going to seduce Kevin?"

"Seduce him?" She blinked stupidly. "Me?"

Sarah rolled her eyes. "Isn't that the point of this weekend? I mean besides Paul getting married of course. The secondary point, then?"

"I thought he'd handle that." The minute the words left her mouth she wished them back. Guys had always been the aggressors in her relationships. This week was about getting out of her rut, not settling back into it in a different place. "No. Forget it. Forget I said that."

"Gladly." Sarah fanned herself. "I thought I was going to have to smack you."

"No, no." Addie took a gulp of champagne punch for strength. Seduce him. *Dear God.*

"I'm thinking tonight you can play a little hard to get, just tease him." Sarah wiggled her fingers gracefully. "And then tonight when everyone is in bed, sneak into his room and *bang*."

The dancing fingers made a vicious grab.

Good Lord. Was she crazy? Just walk into Kevin's room and attack him? Addie pictured him asleep in one of the second-floor bedrooms where Paul and Ellen had put their closest friends. Imagined fitting her naked body to his, waking him with a gentle kiss.

Well.

That would take her pretty damn far out of her rut.

"If I do this…" She shook her head as Sarah started a massive victory dance. "Sarah, I said *if*."

"No chickening out." Sarah waggled a warning finger, eyes flashing excitement. "You can do this. He wants you to, you saw his text and you saw how he greeted you."

"True." Deep inside her, little flutters of excitement, even though the concept was still surreal.

"Come on." Sarah took her arm and dragged her back toward the house. "You need more punch."

A second glass of punch later, Addie and Sarah were in line at the buffet near tables set up in the middle of a circle of tents, loading up on hamburgers, hot dogs, potato chips and bean salad.

"Now we strategize." Sarah surveyed the tables. "We want to sit somewhere empty, not too large, so you can get cozy with Kevin when he comes to join us."

"And you with Joe."

Sarah made a face. "I do not do cozy with Joe. That's Carrie's job."

"Ha. I think if you ever wanted to get cozy with Joe he would be more than happy to."

"What?" Sarah was still analyzing the table situation,

effectively using her habit of blocking out what she didn't want to hear. "Small ones are taken. That one will do."

Addie followed her to a table for six set up at the perimeter of the clearing.

Sarah put down her plate, patting the place diagonally across from her. "You there. Then Kevin can choose if he wants to be intimately close to you on the bench, or to gaze longingly into your eyes across the table."

Addie pretended disgust, giddy inside. "You are a piece of work."

"Aren't I? Hey, Joe." She beamed as Joe sat next to her, and managed to keep the smile going when Carrie sat opposite him.

"May I join you?" Kevin's rich voice—not as deep as Derek's—came from behind Addie's left ear.

"Absolutely." She made a show of giving him room on the bench, then after he was settled, scooted back until their thighs touched. "Isn't it great to—"

"Boy this looks good." He grinned around the table. "Joe, how are you?"

"Not bad." Joe's features turned stiff.

"And you are Carrie?"

"That's me!" Carrie gave a Miss America smile and giggled. She was a tiny redhead from Atlanta, who was so perky and cheerful and enthusiastic about everyone and everything it made Addie want to step on her. "I'm a friend of Ellen's from grade school!"

"Welcome. This is a great gathering. And perfect weather. Supposed to keep going until the ceremony, too. *Hey, Paul.*" Kevin turned, leaning back into Addie, so his shoulder pressed against her breast. He raised his beer to his friend a couple of tables away. *"This one's for you, buddy!"*

Addie turned to see Paul's reaction, but her eyes never

made it that far. Derek, holding a plate and a beer, was making his way…oh, no…straight to their group. Worse, he sat opposite her, where she'd have to look at him.

"Addie, my hot woman." Kevin had turned back to the table and was gazing down at her. "Have I told you how fabulous you look?"

She nodded, laughing. "You have! And then I told *you*—"

"Yeah, I remember now." His eyes skimmed intimately over her. A sudden movement across the table made her glance at Derek, who was giving Kevin another I-would-kill-you-if-it-were-legal glare. Addie turned determinedly back to Kevin, who was still ogling. "You lost a bunch of weight or something, right?"

"Fifteen pounds."

"Good for you. And *you*." Kevin put his elbow on the table, pointing at Derek. "I know you."

"Derek Bates." He said it like a challenge.

"Derek, right. Right." Kevin did a quick drumbeat on the table. "The *s-s-sailor* man."

"And you're the *s-s-sales* man."

Kevin's smile froze slightly. "Vice president of IT sales. Small company but we're making big, big money."

"Impressive." Derek glanced at Addie. "You've known each other a long time?"

"Oh, yeah, Addie and I go way back." Kevin draped his arm casually around her shoulders, and then let it slip across her back and down, landing on what the bench wasn't using of her rear end.

Oh, my.

His hand was warm. His fingers started moving back and forth. She pressed her thighs together experimentally. No, she wasn't dying of lust. But then they weren't in a private room, able to concentrate only on each other and on their feelings.

"We met after Paul and Kevin became friends in middle school," Addie said. "Kevin was—"

"John Witherspoon Middle School in Princeton, New Jersey. Cross-country team. I'd hang out all the time at Paul's house." Kevin leaned in to stage-whisper to Addie. "I always had a crush on you."

She smiled into his gorgeous blue eyes, and then she felt it, a little tingle of chemical connection. Good. It was coming back. For a while she'd worried.

"Nice story." Derek looked as if he'd eaten something that made him sick. The tingle died, and she felt slightly sullied and shamed.

What the heck for? What weird power was this guy starting to have over her? She didn't know, but this had to be the beginning and the end of it.

"Hey, Addie, you ready for a refill on that punch?"

She nodded emphatically. "Definitely. Thanks, Kevin."

"No problem. *Hey, Sarah.*" He shoved Addie's glass toward her. "Addie wants more punch. Could you go get her some?"

Small beat of silence at the table.

"I'm *kidding.*" Kevin laughed; that loud warm laugh that could still make her fizzy, though this time mostly in relief. The rest of the table joined in. Probably not Derek, but Addie couldn't bring herself to check. "I'm getting Addie some punch, do you want some? Carrie? Joe?"

Kevin collected cups and walked off. Addie stared after him, noting the breadth of his shoulders, the elegant tapered line down to slender hips and wiry runner's thighs. She'd have that body next to hers tonight.

Fear and adrenaline hit her hard. She needed more punch. Now. *Hurry, Kevin.*

"Addie."

Derek. She turned reluctantly, dreading what those brown eyes were going to do to her.

Yup. They did.

"What?" She sounded irritable. Because she was.

"You don't have to do this."

She froze, eyes open wide. How did he know about the seduction? Sarah didn't...no, she couldn't have. He couldn't have any idea what he'd just said. She needed to calm down.

"Don't have to do what?"

"Be with this guy if it doesn't feel right."

"I know. I know that." She sounded like a petulant child. "I do."

He pressed his lips together. That grim look again. She wanted to slap it off him. Or kiss—

No.

"Okay." He picked up his plate and his beer. "But I think you're making a big mistake."

"Who's making a mistake?" Sarah turned rather sloppily to stare at Derek. "Addie? What's she doing wrong?"

Addie jerked her head toward where Kevin had gone.

Sarah gasped. "You *told* him?"

"Told her what, what's this?" Carrie was perkily fascinated, "What's goin' on?"

"Addie told me she wants to start a round of female naked cliff diving after dinner." Derek shook his head somberly. "I told her she was making a mistake. We should wait until midnight. And it should be co-ed."

The table erupted into shouts of laughter, then into a cacophony of increasingly bad suggestions.

Addie sent Derek a grateful look. He gave a curt nod and strode over to join Paul's table, where he was immediately pounced on by a blonde big-boobed woman

Paul worked with who was probably incredibly nice—any friend of Paul's had to be—but at that moment Addie hated her. And then herself for caring at all when she had The One That Got Away waiting on her, hand and foot.

"Here we go." Kevin handed drinks around, then sat close to Addie, clinked his beer bottle with her glass and leaned forward to speak privately. "Here's to finding you again, Addie. I think you're a remarkable woman and I look forward to getting to know you again this weekend. I feel like I made a big mistake letting you out of my life."

Ooh. Serious melt. "Thank you, Kevin. That was really sweet. I've thought of you a lot over the years, too."

His grin would be able to charm a cobra. "Cheers."

She clinked with him and raised the glass to her lips, holding his eyes. Definite tingles that time. Big ones. She was transported right back to his car, eleven years earlier, and the way he kissed her, with such sweet reverence, again and again, until passion took them over and turned the kisses hot and breathless.

Sorry, Derek. She'd made up her mind.

Tonight she was climbing those stairs and finishing off eleven years of foreplay.

5

"BEDTIME, JOE." Sarah pointed toward the stairs leading to the Bossons' second floor. She, Joe and Addie were sitting in the living room in front of a fire crackling in the brick hearth, warding off the evening's chill. Other guests were already in bed or on the beach stargazing. Kevin had just gone upstairs, kissing Addie's cheek and smiling meaningfully—maybe?—as he left. Which meant he was probably now in bed. Which meant seduction was imminent.

Addie was terrified.

Joe didn't even glance up from his book. "No way. This is getting good. I can't light the kerosene lamp to read in my room or I'll bother my roommate."

Sarah huffed. "Addie and I have to talk."

"Yeah?" That got his attention. "About what?"

"Girl stuff. Kevin left for bed, your turn now."

Joe snorted. "Kevin was in bed right here. Even my dad doesn't snore that loudly."

Addie cringed. He had been loud. Mouth wide-open, drool glistening in the firelight—not particularly sexually alluring.

"So?" Sarah glanced at Addie then bounced up to stand

an inch from Joe's knees, hands on her hips. "You never snore? The guy traveled today, he had to get up practically in the middle of the night to catch a plane. Now go."

"Okay, okay. I'll go." Joe picked up a bookmark, closed the book and stood, nearly bumping noses with Sarah, who faltered but stood her ground. Addie smiled. *Go, Joe.* He should throw her over his shoulder and take her somewhere private. "But you owe me, Sarah Bosson."

"I do not." She took a step back, wrapping her long black sweater tightly around herself. "Git."

Joe took hold of her arms and planted a lingering kiss on her forehead, waved goodbye to Addie and left, grinning and shaking his head. Addie sighed after him. What she wouldn't give for her own personal Joe. "He's the greatest, Sarah."

Sarah snapped over to look at Addie from where she'd been staring after Joe. "What?"

"Joe." Addie smirked at her. "The best."

"Oh, yeah, he's great." She rubbed her hands briskly together. "So now, Sweet Addie-lide, or should I say, 'Addie-*laid,*' we have plans to make!"

The bottom dropped out of Addie's stomach. "I don't know, Sarah."

Sarah's eyes narrowed. "What do you mean you don't know?"

"I'm not sure this is a good idea."

Sarah threw up her hands. "I *knew* you'd chicken out."

"I am not." She'd been so sure during dinner. Kevin had been so sweet, so attentive, so obviously interested. But it was one thing being on the receiving end of a flirtation and quite another to barge into his room his first night here and demand sex. "I just think…maybe it's bad timing."

"Uh-huh." Sarah tapped her foot, fists planted at her waist. "Try again."

"I'm…having my period."

"Are not."

"I've got a raging case of…whatever."

"Sor-ry," Sarah sang. "You're go-ing."

Addie flopped back on the couch and stared up at the planks of the ceiling. "I don't know, it just doesn't feel right."

"You're chicken."

"I'm *not*—" She lifted her head defiantly then scrunched her face at Sarah's skeptical expression. "Okay, yes, I am, a little. But it's not just that."

"Of course it's just that. How can wild beast seduction feel right if you've never done it before? You have nothing to compare it to. Now." She started pacing the room, braided rug to pine boards to braided rug, *thud thud thud, tap tap.* "You'll want to get in the mood. Obviously sitting here talking to me isn't going to do it. We need to picture the whole thing."

Addie groaned, thinking Sarah was probably right. Jitters were perfectly natural, and this weekend was about throwing off her fears and reaching past her comfort zones.

"I've got it." Sarah went around turning off gas lamps until the room was in semidarkness, lit only by the flickering fire. "That's better. Now close your eyes and think of—"

"England?"

"Kevin."

Addie did close her eyes, but only after rolling them in exasperation. "Okay."

"Now imagine him completely naked." Her voice lowered to a seductive drone. "In bed, waiting for you."

She did. Kevin. Naked. Top to bottom, bottom to toes. Hmm, that wasn't bad. Not at all. "That actually helps."

"Of course it does. Now imagine he has gold skin and just enough body hair to be manly, stopping well short of gorilla."

"I should hope so." She formed a vivid picture. Definitely helping.

"Minimal body fat. Well-defined muscles. Bologna-size schlong."

Addie burst out laughing. "That does *not* help."

"Eyes closed." Sarah waved at her impatiently. "Now imagine yourself naked sliding into bed next to him. Imagine him waking up and touching you everywhere with really good warm hands, kissing you, murmuring incredibly sweet things."

"Yes." Addie smiled dreamily, imagining her little heart out. "That's working."

"Repeat after me, 'I am a sexual goddess.'"

Addie snorted laughter. "I'm who now?"

"Ahem. This will only work if you cooperate."

"Okay, okay." She suppressed a giggle, still enjoying her private naked picture of Kevin. "I'm that, a sexual goddess, whatever."

"With feeling."

"I *am* a *sex*-ual god-*dess!*" She ended the phrase with a ridiculous squeal.

Sarah collapsed onto the couch next to her and folded her arms over her chest. "That's it. You're hopeless."

"Am not."

"Are, too." Sarah punched her shoulder. "You *can* do this, you know."

"Yeah?" Addie turned and looked at her friend, thoughts spinning around a confusing maze of yes-I-will and no-I-won't. Kevin was attracted to her, he obviously wanted her and he might even be harboring feelings for her. So what was the problem?

Maybe she was just chicken. Or maybe she was experiencing a wise instinct warning her away. How could you tell the difference?

One concept kept her from ditching the idea entirely. One very important concept. If she went back to New York without trying to do this, she'd spend forever wondering what would have happened if she had. She'd never get out of her rut if she never took that first big step. Better do it tonight. Get it out of the way so she'd be able to enjoy him and not spend tomorrow nervous all over again.

"Okay." She squeezed her eyes tight shut, then opened one to peek at Sarah. "Okay. I'll do it."

Sarah's head lifted off the couch. "Really?"

Addie nodded, spirits starting to bubble with excitement. "Yes. Really. I'll do it. Now, before I lose my nerve."

"Yay!" Sarah applauded silently. "So what will you do exactly?"

Addie's brave expression slipped. "Exactly?"

"Well, no, not *exactly,* but I mean, like, for example, are you going to go into his room naked?"

"Sarah!" The outrage was automatic, but she did have a point.

"Come on, you have to work out these details."

"You're right." Addie jumped up to start pacing herself. *Thud thud thud, tap tap.* Repeat. "I can't be naked because someone might see me out in the hall."

Sarah got up and started pacing opposite her, doubling the thuds and taps. "So strip in his bedroom, then?"

"He might wake up prematurely."

"Get in bed with clothes on?"

"That's no fun."

They both stopped and stared at each other in dismay.

"Oh!" Sarah started taking off her sweater. "This is perfect. Go up there naked with this wrapped around you.

If someone sees you, you're covered, but once you're in Kevin's room, all you have to do is drop it and voilà, birthday suit."

"That might work."

"Plus you get to feel like Venus on the half shell." She posed, Venus-like, voice high and dreamy, and let the sweater fall. "Letting your garment drop and po-o-ol around your feet."

"Sheer poetry." Addie giggled on her way to their bedroom, already taking off her clothes, nervous and excited—not really in a sexual mood, but that would come later, when the nerves had subsided and she could relax in Kevin's arms.

"Here." Sarah handed the sweater through the door.

Addie finished undressing and draped it around herself then emerged back in the living room and struck what she hoped was a practiced seductress pose. "How do I look?"

"Perfect." Sarah clasped her hands together, beaming. "International woman of mystery. I'm practically hot for you myself."

"Yeah, I wouldn't bother with that."

"Go look." She pointed toward the bathroom they shared.

Addie floated in and peered at herself in the old mirror hanging over the white sink. She did look really good. Her cheeks were flushed, which kept the black material from washing out her complexion. But the dark color made a wonderful sexy contrast to the pale skin of her neck and chest, and plunged dangerously between her breasts.

Her courage rose. She looked like a seductress. No, she *was* a seductress. Not a woman staring at thirty from the bottom of her rut.

She emerged triumphant from the bathroom. "I'm ready."

"Not quite." Sarah brandished a kid's glow stick and bent it to mix the chemicals. The plastic began to glow eerie green.

"Where did you get that?"

"My parents keep a supply in case someone needs a night light. It's going to be pitch-black in his room since there's no moon tonight. You don't want to trip over anything."

Addie cringed at the thought. Nothing would ruin a seduction faster than falling on your face. "You are brilliant, have I ever told you that?"

"Not nearly often enough." Sarah handed over the glow stick. "And it doubles as a great light saber if you want to do battle with random Jedi. You remember where his bedroom is? First on the right?"

"Absolutely."

"Good luck, Addie Baddie." Sarah hugged her tightly. "This is the start of something really wonderful for you. I can just feel it."

A lump rose in Addie's throat. Sarah suspected, but couldn't know how important this was. A chance to change her life. A chance to redeem her mistake with Kevin that night so long ago. A chance to find romance that might really count.

"Thanks, Sarah. I hope so." She kissed her friend's cheek and turned to walk up the stairs, leaving Sarah to sleep alone in the downstairs bedroom they shared.

Kevin Ames.

The wooden stairs creaked sharply a few times; her feet padded across the bare pine boards on the upstairs landing. First bedroom on the right.

She stopped outside the door, closed with an iron latch like all the bedrooms.

Eleven years later, she'd feel that wonderful mouth on

hers again, would feel those strong arms around her, would feel his hand on her breast. And so much more.

Another surge of that odd panic. She closed her eyes, fiercely ordering fear to stop ruining her life. Addie Sewell was going to do this. She deserved this. No matter what happened. Just walking through his door represented a victory—for her and for her future.

Addie reached for the iron handle, pulled the door toward her so the latch would lift silently and walked into the room.

Done!

She closed the door carefully behind her, listening for any sign that Kevin had heard her.

He was still, his breathing slow and even.

She was in.

For a few seconds Addie stood quietly, amazed that she'd actually done this, that she, Princess Rut, had snuck mostly naked into a man's room in order to seduce him, when for years she'd been too scared to say hi to a guy in her elevator.

A sudden calm came over her. This was right.

She took the time to breathe deeply, inhaling Kevin's masculine scent, surprisingly free of beer fumes. He'd had quite a few more than his share. But then this was a celebration weekend. She'd had one glass too many of punch herself.

As silently as possible, she walked toward the bed, glow stick held behind her so it wouldn't be bright enough to wake him. In the dim light she could see a swathe of naked back, his head bent, partly hidden by the pillow.

A rush of tenderness. *Kevin Ames.*

She gently laid the glow stick on the floor, let the sweater, yes, Sarah, pool at her feet, where it covered the stick and reduced the light to the barest glimmer. Addie left it like that. She knew what Kevin looked like. She wanted to feel her way around him, get to know him by touch.

Totally naked now, heart pounding, she climbed onto the edge of the bed then slid down to spoon behind him. His body was warm against hers, his skin soft, his torso much broader than she'd expected. They fit together perfectly.

She knew the instant he woke up, when his body tensed beside hers.

"It's Addie."

"Addie," he whispered.

Addie smiled. She would have thought after all he had to drink and how soundly he'd been passed out downstairs, that she might have trouble waking him.

She drew her fingers down his powerful arm—bigger than she expected. "Do you mind that I'm here?"

He chuckled, deep and low. Addie stilled. She'd never heard Kevin laugh like that.

Before she could think further, his body heaved over and she was underneath him, his broad masculine body trapping her against the sheets. And before she could say anything, gasp or even breathe, he kissed her, a long, slow sweet kiss that made her feel like she was melting into the mattress.

When he came up for air, she knew she'd have to do something. Say something.

But then he was kissing her again. And this time her body caught fire without her permission. She made a funny helpless noise she'd never heard herself make before, and her mouth opened to his kisses and it was all she could do not to open her legs as well and let him inside her right then and there.

Because it was so, so good.

Beyond good.
Unbelievably good.
It just wasn't Kevin.

6

NOW WHAT? ADDIE WAS lying half underneath Derek instead of Kevin, and Derek was kissing her, sweet perfect kisses that reached all the way around her body and pulled her closer to him in every respect. She wasn't exactly objecting.

Which left her with a terribly painful choice to make. Either she could pretend she'd meant to come into Derek's bedroom all along and go through with the seduction, or—

Addie gasped. Derek had started tasting the curve where her shoulder left off and her neck began, sending shivers…everywhere.

This was a time for rational superpowers.

Like this: either continue the seduction, or she could—and should—be honest, tell Derek she was sorry, truly sorry, but she'd made a terrible mistake. And then he'd stop sending her into orbit.

As he'd sent dozens and dozens of other women, all around the world.

That did it.

"Derek." She put up a hand to ward off his next kiss, which he was aiming for her mouth.

"Yes, Addie." He sounded amused. What was so funny?

"Um. The thing is."

"Ye-e-s?" He kissed her bare shoulder, a slow gentle kiss that made her pause, because her shoulder had never been made to feel quite that way and she wanted to enjoy it.

"I made a mistake."

"Really." He lowered his head to her breast; his mouth took her nipple. Wet heat. Pressure. A shock of pleasure through her.

She closed her eyes and forced out her new mantra: other women. Many other women. Probably *all* other women.

"I thought you were Kevin."

He lifted off her very, very disappointed breast. "Yeah?"

Completely unconcerned. Addie blinked up at what she could see of his face. "But—"

Another gasp. His mouth had decided it couldn't neglect her other nipple.

"But…" She struggled to remain coherent. Her hips really wanted to strain toward his, and she needed to get them under control. "I didn't come in here to have sex with you."

"So it seems."

He moved the rest of the way over her. Addie nearly shrieked in protest, until she realized he was wearing underwear. Soft, distended underwear, which was currently transferring amazing amounts of heat to a certain spot between her legs she was very, very fond of.

"But, so that means you need to let me go." No, no, he needed to let her come.

"Does it?" Derek moved his chest back and forth over her breasts, the hair—stopping well short of gorilla—a stimulating male texture across her skin.

Then he started kissing her again in earnest. Powerful

teasing kisses that turned her on as if he was…doing other things. Which she desperately wanted him to be doing.

All of them.

But she'd come in to rekindle something with Kevin, an old friend she could trust with her body and her heart, and it was sort of awful of her to be playing with Derek like he was the shinier, newer toy.

With resolve borne of strength she wished she didn't have, Addie wrenched her lips away from his. "I can't think when you're doing that to me."

"Doesn't that tell you something?"

"Yes. It tells me I can't think when you're doing that to me."

He chuckled and moved back. Immediately her body felt chilly. And lonely. "Better?"

No. "Yes, thank you."

"You're welcome."

Now what? She should get out of this bed immediately, throw Sarah's sweater back on, have whatever conversation they should have while standing safely across the room and then go to bed, after she smacked Sarah silly for giving her the wrong directions to Kevin's room.

"So you were hoping to jump in bed with Kevin. It's not too late, you know. He's right across the hall."

She gaped at him, prickling with outrage. "You think I could make out with you and then go across the hall and seduce Kevin?"

"Why not?" Derek shrugged in the near darkness, lit an eerie Shrek-green shade by the glow stick. He was still sexy. And very unogre-like. "It's not like we exchanged rings."

"No, no, I know, but…" She wasn't sure how to explain it. "I can't. I mean, after this kind of a…connection."

"Connection?"

Argh! What had she used that word for? Thank God for the dim light to hide her blush—but didn't green and red mix to make muddy brown? "No, not that. You wouldn't understand."

"Why not?"

"Because men like you don't." She spoke more harshly than she meant to and swung her legs over the side of the bed, confused, hurt and more confused because she didn't understand why she was hurting. Embarrassed, she'd understand right away. Appalled ditto. But *she* should not be feeling rejected. *She* was the one who'd put a stop to this.

"Hey." His hand scttled on her thigh. His voice was gentle. "I'm sorry. Really. This was a shock to both of us."

"No kidding."

"But the connection wasn't."

She turned to him. Another shock. "You felt that?"

"From the beginning." He drew his hand down her cheek. "I knew we'd be good together."

"Physically." Well, duh, Addie, what did she think he meant, spiritually?

"That much for sure. Don't know what else, yet. You felt it, too."

"I…yes, some. A little. Yeah." Little like the universe was little. "Okay, a lot."

He gave that deep chuckle that had become familiar and very attractive. Like pretty much everything else about him.

In defense, she tried to conjure up a picture of Kevin, and got him snoring and drooling on the sofa.

Oops. But really, that made her feel tenderly toward him for being a normal flawed human being. She might lust after Derek, but tenderness counted for more.

"So tell me, Addie. What did you mean a 'man like you'?"

"Oh." She struggled with how to explain, more aware than she wanted to be that she hadn't left his bed yet, and that it wasn't really difficult to figure out why not.

"One with…considerable experience…in the area of… physical relationships."

Silence for half a beat, then they both started giggling.

"Translation?" he asked lightly.

"Um…you get laid a lot?" That threw them both into another round of suppressed giggles. Very dangerous. Sharing a private joke in bed together made the darkened room seem even more intimate.

"Where did you get that idea, Addie?" He held up his hand. "Wait, don't tell me. Sarah."

"Oh. Well…yes." Addie wrinkled her nose. Sarah, who had lied about him being sexually aggressive on the beach, and whose hobby was inflating gossip. "She said she heard it from Paul."

"Ah." He rubbed his head. "I get it now."

"So…it's true?" Addie bit her lip. Jeez, could she have sounded any more disappointed?

"Paul and I joke a lot about the girl in every port thing. With my career it's hard to have any kind of long-term relationship. I'm never around. But I don't use women, and I don't hunt them just for sex."

Addie drew her knees up, hugged them to her chest, feeling suddenly exposed even though she'd been naked all along. His playboy reputation was the only reason she had stopped her seduction of the wrong man. "You don't ever want to settle down in a real home somewhere?"

"I've thought about it." He pushed hair back that had fallen over her forehead. "But I love what I do. It would take an extraordinary woman to make me want to give up this life."

She nodded, more confused than ever, knowing she

needed to get up and leave and wanting more than ever to lie down in those amazing strong arms and escape into bliss.

What about Kevin?

"So what now, Addie Sewell?" He touched her chin, let his hand fall to the mattress. "Would you like to spend the night with me?"

Yes. She wasn't going to answer that way, but her soul did, loud and clear. "I don't think it's a good idea, Derek."

"No?"

"You're leaving for the other side of the world on Sunday. I don't have to commit to every guy I sleep with, but I generally hope for more than three days."

"And with Kevin you have that option."

"Yes." The answer came out automatically. After what had just happened in this bed, she couldn't picture spending the next three days with Kevin. But she wasn't going to tell Derek that. She needed about a week to sort out her feelings. Why hadn't she stayed home with Great-Aunt Grace's boxes?

"Okay, Addie."

Three beats later, she realized that was her cue. *Bye, Addie, don't let the door hit you...* She slid off the bed and crossed to where Sarah's sweater was covering the glow stick, which burned unpleasantly bright when she slipped the black garment over her shoulders like a cape, wistfully reliving her hope and excitement when she'd let it drop.

Behind her she heard Derek's body swishing over the sheets, then silence. He must have lain down again, and was trying to sleep. Or was he watching her leave? Would he lie awake thinking about her and what might have been? Would she?

At the door, she reached for the handle then heard his footsteps behind her. His arms came up on either side of her head to keep the door from opening, trapping her inside. The sweater fell. She could feel the heat of his body behind her. "Addie."

"Yes." Her voice was a breathless whisper.

"If you change your mind…" His lips landed on her shoulder, stubble a delicious rasp on her skin, making her shiver with desire.

"I will." She froze in horror at what she'd implied. "I mean I *will* let you know."

That gorgeous chuckle again. Then silence so tense she screwed her eyes shut, desperate to leave, but unable to until he chose to let her, desperate to lean back into him and absorb the feel of his skin against hers, to give in, let him take her back to bed and to places she had a feeling she'd never been before.

His arms came down. She was free to go. "Good night, Addie."

"Night." Not bothering to finish covering herself, she grabbed the sweater, pulled the door open and launched herself out into the hall.

Where she collided, butt naked, with the wiry-haired bare chest of Kevin Ames.

7

"Kevin." Addie clutched Sarah's black sweater around herself, covering her breasts, which had obviously been waving around in full view seconds before because Kevin's eyes were still popping out of his head.

"Addie, what…" He gestured past her with his flashlight. "Wait, that's your room? I thought you were sleeping downstairs with Sarah."

"Oh. Uh." God, could this be any worse? "Actually—"

"I thought that was Derek's room."

"It…is." Her stomach gave a sickening lurch. What would have happened if she'd taken the right turn…or rather the left turn? She certainly wouldn't have to be explaining her way out of this mess.

Kevin looked hurt, then angry. "What the hell, Addie? I thought you and I were on to something. Now you're with him?"

"Kevin, we need to talk." Addie pulled him away from the door on the other side of which Derek was undoubtedly laughing his very fine ass off. "Somewhere private."

"Here." He escorted her across the hall and waited expectantly, arms folded, flashlight pointing downward so his face glowed with eerie shadows as well as monster-green from the glow stick.

Addie looked at him questioningly. What was so much more private about this side of the landing? "What about your room?"

"We're fine here. No one will hear us. Why are you coming naked out of this guy's room in the middle of the night?"

"I…" Addie closed her eyes. This was horrible. Since she hadn't made it into Kevin's room, she still had no idea how he might react to the idea of her seducing him. "I thought it was yours."

Kevin was silent for so long, she opened her eyes. Well, one eye. Just for a peek.

His arms were no longer across his chest. He was no longer looking as if he could growl. He looked rather stunned, in fact. "So you slept with Derek instead?"

"No! Of course not." She felt herself blushing in the dim light. It would help nothing to mention how much she'd wanted to sleep with him. "I went in there thinking it was your room and when I realized it wasn't, I came back out."

Just…not quite immediately.

"Addie." His voice was gentle now. "You were going to seduce me?"

"Yes." In sudden horror she realized he could easily say okay, then, let's do it. The only thing she wanted to do less than seduce him now was to explain why she no longer wanted to. She wasn't even sure why herself, except that it had something to do with Derek.

Okay, everything to do with him.

"Wow, Addie. What a surprise." He didn't sound as if he meant a fabulous Christmas-day-biggest-package surprise. More like a so-you've-gone-back-to-drinking surprise. "I didn't think you were the type."

Of course she wasn't. But he didn't need to point that out. "Obviously I'm not. Look how I screwed this up."

"See…to be honest here, Addie, I'm a take-charge kind of guy."

"You are?" She had no idea what he was talking about, and it irritated her. This was Kevin. *Kevin Ames.* Addie was supposed to be melting into a big puddle at his feet, and that was absolutely not happening. Not even close.

Addie, Addie. Be rational. Like this: she was tired, confused, humiliated and so far out of her comfort zone she should probably be wearing an oxygen mask. All she needed was some recharge time, a good night's sleep and a little space to sort through her emotions. Everything would be okay in the morning.

"See, I'm not that into women making the first move."

"Oh." So going into the wrong room and being humiliated had saved her from going into the right room and being humiliated. How nice.

"Yeah, I kind of thought we'd go off alone somewhere, like to a beach or something." He patted her shoulder awkwardly. "Maybe have a few drinks…get to know each other again. Ease into it."

Addie's irritation vanished. Get to know each other again. Yes. *Yes.* She'd been going about this as a theatrical fantasy. Kevin was talking down-to-earth reality. It had been eleven years; they'd both changed and matured. They had a lot of catching up to do, many things to find out about each other as adults. He recognized that, while she'd been planning to jump him his first night here like a horny frat boy.

"Kevin, thank you." Her relief was immense. Re-entry into the comfort zone complete. She covered his hand on her shoulder with hers. "I had put all this pressure on myself and was listening to other people instead of to my instinct and…basically trying to be someone I'm not cut out to be."

"You should never do that, Addie. You want someone who loves you for who you are. You're sweet and adorable. Part of what makes you so sexy is your innocence. You should never try to be anything else."

Addie blinked. She took her hand off his and pulled Sarah's sweater more tightly around herself. He was right about her. Of course he was. But she couldn't help feeling the loss of that moment imagining herself as a wildly sexual seductress.

"Listen." Kevin crossed the distance between them, took her in his arms for a long, comforting hug that—

Oh. Well, now she got the beer fumes. But under them, a nice sweet aftershave that she…pretty much liked. "You go to sleep now. Forget all this. Tomorrow we'll take a walk or something and catch up, okay?"

"Yes." She pressed her cheek against his shoulder. He understood her better than she'd understood herself. "Thank you, Kevin. You're wonderful."

"Aw, I'm just a normal guy, Addie."

Exactly. And that's what she needed and wanted. Her two previous long-term relationships had been solid and comfortable—not dull, but not a passionate thrill a minute, either. She wasn't cut out for that much excitement. It would exhaust her.

"Good night, Addie." Kevin brushed a kiss across her mouth. No wild sparks, just lovely comfort. Which was exactly what she needed just then. He was remarkable.

"Good night, Kevin. Thanks for saving me from myself."

"No problem." He grinned and stayed in front of his

door, watching her descend the steps. At the bottom of the staircase, out of his sight, she heard him open the door to his room—on the *left*—then an odd high whimper, a squeak and a thud. Addie gasped and whirled to stare up into the blackness of the second floor. Had Kevin hurt himself?

A few seconds later, normal footsteps. Addie relaxed and continued into the living room. If he'd been injured, he'd have called her for help. She was not walking into any other guy's room again on this vacation unless she was sure she was invited.

In fact, all she wanted to do was sneak into her room, and drop into a dead sleep.

She passed the glowing embers of the fire, used the bathroom and came back into the living room to stare out the window at the water. It was peaceful and contented tonight, reflecting the brightest stars in two glittering lines across its gentle waves.

So beautiful. So uncomplicated. She could learn a lot from an ocean.

At her room's door, she stopped, put firm, careful pressure on the latch and eased the door open.

Dark. Quiet. Soft steady breathing from Sarah. Addie wilted in relief. The last thing she wanted was to have to explain any of the bizarre comedy of tonight's errors to her friend.

She crept into the room, laid the glow stick on the small table next to her twin bed and fumbled under her pillow for her pajamas. Sleeping naked was sexy with a man, but alone it felt all wrong and cold.

Sarah's sweater dropped off her easily; her pajamas bottoms went on easily. But when she swung her arms after pulling on the tops, she bumped the table and knocked the glow stick to the floor. Not only did it hit the boards with a bang, but it rolled noisily before she could grab it.

"...Addie?"

Argh!

"Hi, Sara-a-ah," she whispered soothingly. "Don't wake up...I'm just going to bed."

"Don't wake up?" Sarah was already up on her elbows, eyes wide, turning on the electric lamp next to her bed. "How can I possibly sleep? What happened? Why are you back so early? Tell me everything."

Good Lord, zero to sixty in two seconds. "In the morning, Sarah, I'm exhaus—"

"What do you mean morning? Are you kidding me? I'll go out of my mind." She tossed aside half the covers and patted the mattress next to her. "C'mon. Spill."

Addie sighed. If she wanted any sleep tonight, she'd have to tell everything. Otherwise Sarah would be at her until the end of time. She crossed reluctantly and sat next to her friend; let Sarah fuss putting the covers back over their legs.

"Now, tell."

"Okay." Addie blew out a breath. "First off all, Sarah, Kevin's room is on the *left* at the top of the stairs."

"No, it's not. It's on the—" Her eyes shot wide. She slapped a hand over her mouth. "Omigod. Omigod."

"Yeah."

"But if you turned right...wait, *did* you turn right?"

"Oh, yes."

"So you went into—" She gasped. "Derek's room!"

"Yup."

"You walked in and took off your clothes in *Derek's room?*"

"Uh-*huh.*"

"No!" She gave a strangled yell that could have been

laughter but probably wasn't. "Tell me you didn't climb into bed with him."

"I did."

"Oh, God! At least tell me he threw you out right away or you bolted. At least tell me he didn't touch you."

Addie turned to look at her incredulously. "Uh, Sarah?"

"He *did*." The wail was anguished and unexpected. "I knew it."

"For heaven's sake." Apparently any contact between her and Derek was highly offensive to everyone tonight. "I apologized, we talked for a couple of minutes and I left the room."

Sarah was nearly in tears. "I'm sorry. I am being ridiculous. It's just that you always…"

"Always what?"

"Get the guy!"

"Sarah!" Addie was more stunned at that moment than she'd been all evening. And it had been one hell of an evening. A vision of her neat and ordered rooms in Aunt Grace's apartment floated temptingly. Maybe she wouldn't get a condo. Maybe she'd stay there forever with her lovely routines and cats, flossing regularly, and never change anything in her life ever again. "I didn't 'get' Derek. I don't even want him. And I have no idea who else you could mean."

"Kevin."

"Wait, you want Kevin?"

"No!" Sarah wailed.

Addie pressed a hand to her temple. This was going to make her insane. "Do you want me to finish the story?"

"Yes." She sniffled. "I'm sorry."

"Okay. So I charged out of Derek's room, still pretty much naked, and I bumped into Kevin. Literally."

Sarah gaped at her. Let the record show that for once Addie had managed to render her speechless.

"You. Did. *Not*."

Speechless at least for one second. "I did. And you know what? When he found out I'd been going to seduce him, he said he'd rather get to know me again slowly first."

Another gasp. "Oh, Addie! That is adorable. I knew you and Kevin were right for each other. Derek is seriously bad news."

For a weird second Addie wanted to defend Derek. Quite hotly. But that would get her exactly nowhere. Besides, she had no proof that Derek wasn't a player, just Sarah's word, which, depending on Sarah's mood, might or might not mean anything.

"So now you and Kevin are good?"

"We're good." Actually Addie had no idea what they were, but she smiled and squeezed Sarah's leg anyway by way of saying good-night, and got up, completely drained, not wanting to think about Derek or Kevin or any combination thereof for the rest of the night if not weekend. Sarah turned off her lamp and Addie got into bed by the nauseating green light of the glow stick, which she never, ever wanted to see again.

"Addie? Are you going to go after Derek now?"

Addie paused, about to bury the offending light under her pillow. What the hell was she talking about? "Of course not. Why, do *you* want to go after him?"

"Me? *Me?*" Sarah laughed loudly. "As if. I would never go after a player like that. His criteria for choosing a sex partner is female and breathing. No, no, I was just worried you'd get hurt."

"Okay, then." Addie sighed, feeling like she'd been hollowed out and filled with sadness. Maybe she'd give up this whole man thing. At least for now. It had all become way too complicated.

"Hey, Addie. I had a great idea."

Addie groaned. "If this has anything to do with men, I don't want to hear it."

"Aw, Addie. C'mon. You…" Silence, while Addie could practically hear the wheels turning in her head. "No, nothing about men, it's to cheer you up."

"Go ahead." Addie yawned and nestled into the pillow, immediately having to banish memories of lying nestled against Derek.

Oh, dear.

"There's a secret cove on Storness Island. No one knows about it but our family. The entrance to the path is camouflaged and you can't see the beach from the water, either, because there's a spit of land in the way. Let's go there and sunbathe nude tomorrow. Take a break from guys and everything…."

"Sure," Addie murmured drowsily. Sarah was up to something, but right then she didn't have the energy to care. "Fine. Whatever."

"It's great, you'll love it."

"Mmm…"

She was asleep in about ten seconds. When she woke up, she was sorting boxes in Great-Aunt Grace's old bedroom, patiently and meticulously organizing the contents, letters here, photographs there, all spread out on Aunt Grace's four poster bed.

Where suddenly Derek was lying naked, smiling devilishly.

Impossible. He didn't know where Aunt Grace lived. He was in Maine.

A blink later, she was naked in bed with him, but not at Aunt Grace's anymore, he was back in Maine, and she was kissing him ravenously until her body caught fire. Literally. And then Kevin was in bed with them, too, not seeming to mind the heat, making odd sucking sounds through his lips. Derek, not at all fazed by the bed being in flames, kicked with incredible power and sent Kevin flying across the room, where he curled up fetal and was instantly covered with seaweed, dribbling sand and water onto the braided rug.

Awestruck, Addie looked up at Derek, looming over her, the two of them within a circle of fire now, like Siegfried and Brünnhilde from Wagner's Ring cycle, which her parents had dragged her to as a teenager over her violent objections.

You are mine, Addie. You know it as well as I do. We belong together. I felt it the second I met you, and you did, too. Kevin isn't fit to wash your underwear.

The dream changed and slowed. The fire was gone, the bed, clean and white again, floated on the sea, rocking gently, blue water all around, white clouds overhead, sweet breezes blowing it toward the sunset. What didn't change was the passionate heat in Derek's eyes, and the figurative fire in her body.

He moved over her, and kissed her. She spread her legs and he slid inside her, his motion echoing the rocking of the bed and the waves, making love to her in time to nature's rhythm, back and forth, in and out...

As her arousal grew fierce, Addie began waking up.

No, no. Not yet, not yet!

She kept her eyes shut, keeping out reality, holding on to the feel of Derek's body on top of hers. Her hand crept between her legs. In her mind she was still with him, out on that bright sea, tasting the salty breeze on his skin, moving her hips in time with his, feeling him moving deep inside her.

Her fingers rubbed faster, then faster. The orgasm hit her hot and hard, alone in the dark.

Derek Bates.

Kevin Ames.

What the hell was she going to do?

8

DEREK LIFTED THE ax high into the air and brought it down with a satisfying *thunk*. The small birch log split neatly down the middle; he added the pieces to the good-size stack he'd already cut. That morning he'd run twice around the island, done a punishing calisthenics workout, taken a ball-shrinking dip—couldn't really call it swimming, more like flailing, splashing and gasping—in the icy sea, and was now involved in chopping enough wood for the Bossons to burn for the next twenty summers.

Hey, he was happy to help them out. Less charitable was the fact that every time the ax bit deeply into the wood, he was imagining Kevin Ames's head.

Thunk.

Last night he'd barely slept after Addie left.

For one thing, he couldn't erase the feel of her. The softness of her skin, her lips, the gentle swell of her breasts, the warm length of her body under his.

From the first shock of discovering her in his bed, he'd suspected she'd made a mistake. Last night at dinner she'd made it quite clear that she was still determined to go after Kevin. God only knew what kind of Freudian slip brought her to his bed instead, but he didn't believe for a second it was only an accident. Somewhere deep in her subconscious, Addie had known exactly what she was doing. For that reason Derek had no qualms about trying to prove she was in the right place with the right man.

He'd almost succeeded, too. Together they'd generated serious hunger and heat. But while he wasn't above a little underhanded persuasion, he wasn't going to tie her down and force her to stay.

Thunk.

Ha. Derek had thought letting her go was agony. No, he'd tasted true agony when he realized she'd walked out of his door straight into the arms of the man she'd intended to have all along. He'd stood there, incredulous, still smelling her scent on his skin, listening to them talk for a few seconds before he moved away, not interested in hearing anything they were saying, not wanting to think about what might happen next.

Thunk.

Could Addie respond to him the way she had and then jump into bed with Kevin? He'd sure as hell like to think not. Whatever was between Addie and himself, whether it was simple chemistry or something deeper, he'd never experienced anything close to it. And he'd be willing to bet by Addie's clear struggle between wanting out of his bed and wanting to stay in it, that she'd been surprised and overwhelmed by their passion, as well.

So now what? Spend the next three days watching her throw herself at a drunken jerk who wouldn't let her finish a sentence or express a thought? A guy Derek had caught the day before flirting outrageously with Carrie, who'd been puppy-dogging after Joe, who was tagging after Sarah, who was still semi subtly presenting herself to Derek, who was going crazy for Addie, who wanted Kevin?

Thunk.

If Addie was trying to land a really great guy, it would still be hard to step aside, but Derek wouldn't hesitate. He had nothing to offer a woman long-term but a nomad's life on the sea or a lonely life in port, waiting for him to come home. There were undoubtedly some women out there who'd embrace that life, but Addie had spelled out quite clearly that she wasn't one of them. Nor was she the type to enjoy the here and now and to hell with later.

He laid the ax across the stump he'd been using as a chopping pedestal, enjoying the faint breath of breeze across his bare torso. Hot day. At this rate he might make it back into the ocean for more ball-shrinking fun.

"Hey, Derek." Incredibly the object of his ax-wielding fury strolled into the clearing and lifted his fist for a bump. Derek hated fist bumps. "Puttin' in some good sweat there, huh?"

"Yeah."

Kevin put his hands on his hips and slouched into a casual pose, apparently settling in to watch. He was wearing plaid shorts. Derek hated plaid shorts. With a yellow polo shirt. Derek hated yellow.

"Nice day." Kevin yawned wide and long, without covering his mouth.

"Rough night?" Derek couldn't help himself, even knowing he should shut the hell up.

"Man, yeah. Crazy night." Kevin laughed, scratching his head enthusiastically. "Amazing night."

Derek picked up the ax, sweat turning cold, stomach sinking. Addie had gone from his bed to Kevin's.

No, he couldn't believe she'd do that. Did that make him perceptive or in denial?

"That girl is a gymnast." He put his hands to his lower back and bent side to side. "Wore me out."

That girl? Derek's grip tightened on the handle. Did he forget her name already? With the amount Kevin had to drink last night, Derek wouldn't be surprised. Though until he heard that Kevin had for sure been with Addie, he wasn't going to believe it. Not totally. She was an intelligent, passionate, exciting woman, and Kevin…wore plaid shorts. "Congratulations."

"Yeah, thanks." He yawned again. "Have you seen Addie around this morning?"

Derek blinked. Something about the way Kevin emphasized her name—as if he'd been talking about someone else before—gave him some hope. "Not lately."

"Thought I'd see if she wanted to go on a walk with me this morning."

"Yeah?" He hauled up the blade for his next swing, trying to look as casual as possible. "When did you last see her?"

Thunk.

"In the middle of the night." Kevin smirked. "Guess she paid you a visit by mistake first."

Derek held Kevin's gaze. Very bad idea to taunt a man holding an ax. "She spent some time in my room, yeah." *Not sure she thought it was entirely a mistake.*

Kevin's turn to look uncomfortable. "Well, I haven't seen her this morning."

Damn it. Still no definite answer. She might not have spent the whole night with him.

Sarah sprang into the clearing holding a towel around herself, cheeks rosy, body glistening. She stopped short when she saw the two men, then her eyes lit up and she pursed her lips as if about to whistle. "Well, gentlemen, hello."

"Are you naked under there?" Kevin's eyes were practically shooting out of their sockets.

Derek snorted. Didn't the guy ever listen to himself? "I think what he meant was, 'Hi, Sarah, great to see you.'"

"That's what I thought." Sarah spared Derek a glance then turned to Kevin. "Addie and I were sunbathing in the altogether."

"Where?" Both men spoke at once then glared at each other.

"Ha!" Sarah snapped her fingers at each of them. "Like I'd tell you?"

"Okay." Kevin turned to Derek, all pretend business. "We'll split up. You take that way, I'll take this way, we'll search the island."

Hilarious, Kevin.

"Yoo-hoo!" Carrie bounced into the clearing, beaming. The woman made Sarah look low-energy and depressive. She sent Kevin a slow, sexy wink that made Derek straighten up and take notice. *"There* you are."

"I'm here." Kevin laughed nervously, looking from Sarah to Derek and back.

Well, well. Wasn't *that* interesting.

"Hi, Sarah!" Carrie gave a cute little finger-wiggle at Sarah who gave an even cuter finger wiggle back, wearing a gruesomely overbright smile, which went right over Carrie's head.

"And hel-*lo, Derek.*" She looked him up and down in a way that made him want to put his shirt back on. "You are lookin' fine this morning."

"Derek's helping the Bossons out with their firewood supply," Kevin said. "I was about to take over."

Like hell.

"So, Kev-i-i-n." Carrie sashayed over to him, and tiptoed her fingers up his arm, sticking her face up close to his. "How's my wild man this morning? You tired from last night or ready for more?"

The last sentence came out in a stage whisper that everyone heard. Kevin's face turned cranberry-red. He stuttered out a few syllables. Somehow Derek managed not to pump his fist and shout, *yes!*

Sarah froze and blinked at Carrie, then at Kevin. Then back. Her eyes narrowed into furious slits. "What the hell is going on here?"

"What?" Carrie gaped at her in wide-eyed surprise. "Oh, no. Y'all aren't dating him are you?"

"*No,* I'm not dating him."

"So what's the problem?" She looked so bewildered Derek nearly felt sorry for her. But yesterday she'd been all over Joe, now Kevin, so he doubted she cared much for anyone but herself.

"Uh, so, Carrie." Kevin pried her fingers off his biceps. "What are your plans this morning?"

Carrie beamed and tucked her arm all the way through his. "Whatever *you're* doing."

"You know, Kevin, in case you feel like a long walk…" Sarah smiled with dangerous sweetness. "There's this short pier on the other side of the island."

Kevin had the sense to look mortified.

"Ooh, maybe we'll do that." Carrie pulled him around, clearly missing the insult, which Derek remembered as one of Sarah's father's favorites. "Come on, Kev. See y'all later!"

The second the two of them disappeared between the trees, Sarah abandoned all pretense at civility. "What the hell was that?"

Derek did everything he could to look appalled and furious, but he was ready to sing hallelujah. Not only had Addie *not* been with Kevin last night, Kevin had shown his true colors to Sarah, who would waste no time passing the information along to her best friend. And that would very nicely take care of Kevin. "Looks like they're an item."

"He was supposed to be with *Addie* last night."

"Addie was exactly where she was supposed to be."

Sarah glared at him, then stalked over and poked him in the chest. "Listen to me."

He caught her finger. "Hey. Hands off the merchandise."

"You listening to me?"

He suppressed a smile. He liked Sarah. "I'm listening."

"Why didn't you sleep with me that night? No bullshit."

"Because you were drunk, because you're my best friend's sister and because I had nothing to give you beyond that one night. No bullshit."

She was quiet awhile, digesting that. Actually he'd never seen her hold so still. "So are you really not a player?"

"I'm not." He held her gaze. "Never had the time or inclination."

"Why did I overhear my brother talking as if you were?"

Derek kept himself from rolling his eyes. That again. "Because he likes the cliché of sailors. Woman in every port, ha-ha-ha. It's our little joke. Not very funny, but we're guys. We like that stuff."

Sarah nodded, still frowning, but clearly calmer. Derek picked up his shirt and put it back on. He was done chopping wood.

"You like Addie don't you?"

"I do." He was surprised by the question, surprised by his immediate answer and by the emotion in his voice. Yes, he liked her. Against all logic, a woman he barely knew, he liked her a whole hell of a lot.

Sarah twisted her lip. Started to speak, changed her

mind. Folded her arms across her chest and glared at him some more.

He gave her a brotherly punch on the shoulder. "Spit it out, Sarah."

"Hey. The merchandise!"

"Sorry." He raised his hands in surrender. "Truce?"

Her expression softened. "Okay, truce."

"Good." He risked a smile and actually got a warm one back. "Now what were you going to tell me?"

"There's a hidden cove on this island."

"Yeah?"

"One you can't get to unless you know where to find the entrance. It's a total family secret."

"I see." He didn't yet, but was willing to be patient.

"Addie's still there."

Derek eyed her warily, not sure what she was getting at. "Okay."

"Naked."

He swallowed and said the only thing he was capable of: *"Glrmph."*

"Listen to me. Pay close attention." Sarah leaned closer, blue eyes direct and no-nonsense. "Because I'm only going to say this once."

SARAH SAT ON the ledge near her favorite rock, a white crystalline boulder dropped in the middle of jagged gray granite, as if the gods had been playing sky golf and lost track of one ball. At high tide the rock was near-covered, but now it sat exposed in all its glory.

Newly slathered with SPF 50 after sunbathing with Addie, loving this stretch of sunny days after the fog and clouds earlier in the week, Sarah was shucking corn. Forty ears, in preparation for the rehearsal dinner that night. The bag of unshucked sat to her right, the paper shopping bag for husks on her left. The naked ears, she was laying in the family's huge midnight-blue enameled pot with white specks she'd always thought looked like snow. They'd use the pot again to cook lobsters for the wedding feast the following night, when weather forecasters predicted more perfection. Paul and Ellen deserved nothing less.

From the clearing where she'd confronted Derek and learned the truth about Kevin's snakelike character, Sarah had gone straight to the house and volunteered for a job, needing a steadying task. She still couldn't believe Kevin, the guy she was so sure would find love with Addie, the guy she and Addie had been so crazy about for so many years, was a complete jerk.

She ripped off a handful of husks, threw them in the bag. And she still couldn't believe she'd told Derek where to find naked Addie. *Derek!* The guy she wanted. The guy she'd lusted after for years, pined after for many point-less hours, hoping this week that she could finally change his mind.

Pointless. She could see that now so clearly. Maybe she'd finally gotten sick of all the years chasing men when that one crucial concept was missing: them wanting her, too. Maybe she was growing up. Definitely she was ready to string Kevin up by his balls and she was ready to change her opinion of Derek. Definitely she was trying to be happy for Derek and Addie, even if they only had through Sunday together. She and Addie had talked that morning and it was pretty clear to Sarah that Addie was smitten with Derek, even as she'd tried to pretend Kevin still had a chance. Funny how you could figure out other people's crap much more easily than your own.

Kevin. And *Carrie!* Jeez. How typically male. Sarah rubbed an ear free of the last few strands of silk. Though, really, in her new mood of analytical maturity, she should examine that statement, too. What was a typical male? Not fair to say Clueless Neanderthal. Paul wasn't like that. Joe wasn't like that. And now it seemed Paul had been right all along and Derek wasn't like that, either. So there were exceptions. She just couldn't seem to fall in love with exceptions. Look what she did with Derek the second she realized he was a good guy—gave up on him immediately and handed him over to her best friend. And she should have known immediately that if she'd wanted Kevin at some point, he must be bad news.

A strand of silk escaped the garbage and flew on a welcome puff of breeze toward the water. Following it with her eyes, she saw Joe coming toward her, striding easily across the rocky beach, hair wet and tousled. Joe would understand. He'd listen. He'd tease her if she was being ridiculous and support her if she wasn't.

She should really work on falling in love with Joe.

"Hey, Sarah. I've been sent to help you."

Sarah beamed at him and gestured to the ledge. "Pull up a rock."

"As soon as I find one that fits." He tried a few places, attempting the difficult task of getting the shape of the human butt to match comfortably with the craggy formations. "There."

"Just showered?"

"I went swimming."

Sarah gaped at him. "What are you, a polar bear?"

"Warm day." He picked up an ear and started working with her. "Sure cooled me off in a hurry."

"The breeze should pick up in a minute. The tide is changing."

"Yeah?" He glanced at her admiringly. He looked handsome today. The bit of sun on his face helped brighten his complexion, heightened his cheekbones. "How can you tell?"

"Lobster buoys." She pointed at the nearest, yellow and white striped. "They point out when the tide's going out, in when it's coming in. Right now they're starting to swing around."

"Cool."

She added a corn ear to the pot and wiped her hands on her shorts. Time to confess, since she confessed pretty much everything to this man. "Joe?"

"Sarah?"

"I'm afraid I've done a terribly unselfish thing." She sighed dramatically. "It's awful."

"Sarah, I'm so sorry." He picked up on the game right away, features contorting with worry. "How can I help?"

"I don't know. I've never done anything like this before." She pressed diva-fingers to her temple and closed her eyes. "I think I'm in shock."

"No!" He gasped comically. "What did you do?"

"Believe it or not, I'm about to tell you." She opened her eyes and resumed her normal voice. "I realized Kevin is a complete A-hole. But Derek is a good guy."

"Agreed on both counts."

"Yeah, well." Sarah shrugged. "Took me a while to figure it out."

"You should have asked me. I know everything."

"Uh-huh." She took his corn and added it to the pot, tore more husks from her own. "I also decided it was stupid to hold out hope for Derek."

"Really?" He stopped with his hand in the bag of corn, dark eyes clear and watchful. "You gave up on him? Really?"

"Yes." She let out another heaving sigh, enjoying her role tremendously. "Completely."

"Why?"

"Because, Joe." Sarah smiled sadly, feeling wise and old, and the way Joe was looking at her, maybe lovely, too. "He didn't want me."

"The fool."

"And there's more."

"Sarah…" He cringed, putting a hand to his chest. "I'm not sure my heart can take this."

"I gave him a green-light push toward Addie just now. He really likes her and she really likes him."

"Wow, Sarah. That was a really generous thing to do." He tsk-tsked, eyes twinkling. "You must feel terrible."

"I should." She wrinkled her nose, surprised by what she was about to say. "But I don't. I feel sort of glad for them. And sort of relieved."

A slow smile spread over Joe's face, making him even more attractive. Maybe it was the light? The beautiful Mainescape around them? "I'm speechless."

She nodded, proud inside, but not wanting to be gross about it. Joe's approval meant a lot to her. For nearly ten years since she met him when he stepped in to help her out with a cranky customer at the campus bookstore, their friendship had consisted of Joe being a steady, stable source of comfort and support, while she flailed and wailed and stumbled through life.

"Joe?"

"Sarah?"

She frowned down at her next ear of corn. "What do you get from this friendship with me?"

"Uh. I— Huh?"

She giggled. Maybe he could be a clueless male, too. "I mean, you give me total acceptance, unconditional support, lifts and reality checks when I need them. What do I give you?"

"Aw, Sarah…" He tossed husks toward the garbage. They missed and fell onto a sandy patch below the ledge.

"I'll get them." They spoke together, both scrambling down to pick them up, each gathering half. He didn't answer her smile with his usual bright one. Looked down at his feet. Out to sea. She shouldn't have asked him the question.

"You don't have to answer, Joe." Especially if his answer was, *You bring me nothing.*

"I don't have the words right yet."

Sarah bit her lip, feeling queasy. "Tactful phrasing required?"

"No." He took the husks from her hand, tossed them into the garbage bag and came back to stand in front of her, looking down at her earnestly. "Risky phrasing."

"What do you mean?" Sudden fear. She knew what was coming. A truth she'd denied for years because it suited her to. God, why was she seeing everything so clearly today? Couldn't she space it all out a little? She wanted to turn and run back to the cove, interrupt Addie and Derek and tell them sorry, but she changed her mind and they had to have a threesome immediately.

Then Joe did something she'd never seen him do. He changed. He got taller and broader and more muscular and more masculine. Before her eyes. She couldn't breathe.

He took her hand, put it to his lips then pressed it to his heart. "You are loyal and generous and you make me laugh and cry and suffer and celebrate and always, always hope."

Sarah's breath went in as if it would never stop. No one had ever said anything that lovely and romantic to her. Ever.

"Joe, that was so beautiful," she whispered.

The breeze she'd predicted sprang up, playing with his now-dry hair, sending strands of hers across her face. For one terrifying moment, she thought this new version of Joe was going to kiss her. He had that look in his eye, one she'd seen plenty of times, but never on Joe. The predatory my-woman look.

No, no, no, not Joe, that wasn't right, he wasn't—

Oh, dear. He was.

Would she let him? No! She wasn't ready!

God took care of her. The breeze strengthened and knocked over the garbage bag, spilling husks everywhere. By the time they got those cleaned up and went back to their work, Joe was himself again, the moment was over, and they were back to being comfortable friends.

Almost. Sarah couldn't quite forget. For that one second the thought of kissing Joe had been terrifying, yes. But also just the tiniest bit…thrilling.

And maybe, if she allowed herself to think about it—absolutely right.

ADDIE WOKE UP, bleary-eyed and cranky and very, very sandy. What time was it? Where was she? What was she—

Right. Storness Island. The secret cove. She'd been there all morning with Sarah. They'd had a long conversation analyzing the world and all men in it, noting particularly how unworthy way too many of them were.

That part was mostly Sarah.

Addie struggled to sit up, brushing back a tangle of hair. Then they'd moved on to discuss, specifically, Kevin, Derek and Joe, and how maybe Sarah had been wrong about Derek. And how Addie should give him a chance as well as Kevin and see what happened because you couldn't have enough eggs in different baskets.

That part was mostly Sarah, too.

After she left, insisting Addie stay on for a good while to relax, Addie had been exhausted. Give Derek a chance this weekend? *And* Kevin? The woman who'd been tempted to spend this week filing? Please.

Since the day was hot, she'd retreated to a banana shaped spot at the edge of the beach, where bushes and vegetation had formed a sheltering canopy, and covered herself with her towel. Apparently she'd kicked it off at some point while she was asleep and, just as apparently, a warm breeze had come up and blown more sand on her, plus the sun had moved and taken away a lot of the shade. So now she was naked, sweaty, thirsty and probably a little sunburned.

She stood up groggily and shook out her towel in the stiffening breeze, eyes squeezed shut and head turned, then tried to brush the sticky sand off her sticky body.

Ouch. Sand grains brushing over sunburned skin equaled sandpaper. Addie looked longingly toward the water. A skinny promontory and a kind of zigzag in the island's coast formed a natural pool that looked perfect for swimming, and hid whoever was in the cove from passing boats. The tide was low now, but should be on its way in. Sarah told her the best time for swimming was sunny days when high tide had been creeping up over pre-heated sand and rocks all afternoon. This water wouldn't be warm, but it would get this sand off more effectively and a lot less painfully.

She marched down the beach, which was relatively steep so the tide hadn't gone out that far, and gingerly stepped in.

Brrrr. Cold. Especially on heated skin.

She stuck her other foot in.

Really cold.

This would take considerable courage, but if Addie did a superfast wash-off of sand and sweat, her body would feel great when she was back in the warm sun again.

She hoped.

Another step, and another, until she was up to her knees, then thighs, then…*oh* that was cold. Men would *not* want to do this. Not if they wanted to have children someday.

A few more steps and the coarsening sand under her feet turned to pebbles, then rocks. She had to pick her way carefully, testing with her feet to be sure stones were stable before trusting them with her weight.

It would be much easier to swim.

In past her waist, she paused, swirling her hands in the greenish depths, following shafts of sunlight picking up tiny particles, not unlike sunbeams shining through dust or mist.

So. This swimming thing. She needed to dive in and get it over with.

Ready?

One. Two. Three. *No!*

Chicken.

One more step, then she'd dive for sure. Addie stepped bravely forward onto a stone that toppled and threw her. She shrieked and fell, tried to regain her footing, floundered, then lost the bottom entirely and went under. She flailed to the surface, treading water, gasping, already turning so she could get back to shore as fast as possible. One long stroke in, she got the bottom back under her feet. Whew. Another step and she stumbled and fell again into what she had now decided was fresh iceberg melt. Feet scrambling, she fell twice more, sputtering and shrieking, before she finally reached sand and stability in waist-high water, so she could stagger safely back to—

Derek.

Oh, my God.

Derek was standing on the beach, feet spread, hands on his hips, grinning.

Her eyes shot open about as wide as they could go; her hands sprang to cover her breasts. Thank God water was still covering…the rest.

What the hell was he doing here? Sarah said no one knew about the cove. How did he find her? What was she going to do? Why was he standing there staring at her?

Her teeth started to chatter.

She was *naked* and the water was *freezing.*

"Uh. Hi, Derek."

"Hi, there."

She wanted to growl at his cheerfulness. "Um, could you turn around so I can go get my towel?"

"Nope." He was enjoying himself, the rat.

"Nope? What do you mean nope?"

"What do you think?" He walked forward a few steps and guess what, did some more grinning and staring.

Damn it, Derek, this was not fair.

Time for her rational superpowers. Like this: she could run for her towel, giving him only a speeding peek, which might not be all that terrible considering he'd had his hands all over her last night.

Or she could just say to hell with it and walk to her towel at a normal pace, letting him know she was not ashamed or embarrassed about her body. Yes, okay, her hands were currently cemented over her breasts, both of which were joining the rest of her body in being covered with oh-so-not-sexy goose pimples, but she'd chalk that up to panic and forgive herself.

Once covered, she'd be in a good position to discuss whatever he was here to discuss. Or whatever she wanted to discuss. Like maybe that she and Sarah had talked about—

Addie gasped.

Derek was walking deliberately toward her. *Prowling*

was a better word, because his intentions were quite clear in his expression and in the animal way his body was moving. Everything about him was broadcasting what she'd felt from him last night in bed.

I want you.

Oh, help. Addie had to run for the towel *now,* while she could still feel her legs.

The water covered Derek's feet. He didn't even flinch.

His ankles were gone now.

His shins.

Go! Now!

She wasn't moving.

Why wasn't she moving?

Move!

There! Good! Now she was moving!

But *wait,* what was wrong with her, she was not walking toward her towel, she was walking toward *him!*

Stop, before it's too late!

Four feet away from him her hands dropped from her breasts to her sides.

It was already way too late.

9

ADDIE KEPT WALKING. She walked straight into Derek's arms, naked, dripping wet and salty, and she kissed him. Hard.

What was she doing?

Something utterly, deliciously and completely spontaneous.

What about Kevin? What about how he wanted to get to know her slowly, see if they could have something real together?

Addie's lips faltered, then it hit her. She didn't want Kevin. The moment she'd seen him she'd known. The only reason she'd been hanging on to the idea of reconnecting was that it was her *plan* and God forbid Addie Sewell not stay the course and go through with one of her plans.

Derek's arms came around her, and he kissed her back. And how.

But this man has nothing to offer. He'll be back at sea in a few days.

Nothing to offer? She pressed herself against him, felt a rather impressive swelling in his shorts. Seemed to her he had *plenty* to offer.

And guess what? She was taking it. And that made her, right now, about the wildest she'd ever been.

Addie turned off the voice in her head and gave herself over to what she was feeling. Warm, soft lips taking hers, warm hands stroking the line from her waist to her hip. Warm sun and breezes drying her skin. And hot, hot longing throughout her whole body.

She'd never felt like this, never experienced this overwhelming and desperate need. Not for anyone ever.

"Addie." He led them out of the water, working as hard as she was to control his breathing. "Shouldn't we talk about—"

"No." She took hold of his shirt and pulled him back to her. The feel of the fabric under her fingers became annoying. She wanted skin.

Up came his shirt; she helped him drag it over his head and oh, my goodness, what a chest. It should be on permanent display at a treasure chest museum.

Her hands fumbled at the button on his shorts, got them open, unzipped, down. No underwear. Oh, my goodness. That part of him should be on display at the rock-hard hall of fame.

Hard because of her, and this incredible want they generated together.

He pulled her close, pressing her body against his, and oh, the sensations were incendiary, exciting…and not enough. *Not enough.* She wanted more of him, all of him. *Now.*

Good Lord, what kind of wanton creature had she turned into?

The best kind. She'd never felt so primal, so real, so… herself. No expectations, no role to fill, nothing but what her body wanted and needed.

Even if she and Derek lasted only a few days, this new

sense of herself and her power would forever be hers, Derek's gift to her, lasting until death.

She lifted her leg to wrap around his hip; he reached down to stroke the softness between her legs. Addie moaned and clutched his shoulders, distantly aware of the gurgling swish of the waves and the occasional call of gulls. Beautiful spot. Beautiful man.

And speaking of beautiful spot. His fingers…

Too soon he stopped and spanned her waist with his strong hands, preparing to lift her. She grabbed him around the neck and gave a little hop into his arms to help him, though he could probably have lifted her without it.

Mmm…

Kissing her—open, wet kisses that were making her lose her mind—he walked her up the beach then set her on her feet by a towel he must have brought with him. How long had he been there watching her before she noticed him?

"Wait here." He strode back toward the shorts he'd dropped on the beach.

She giggled, pushing hair back from her face. "Like I'd leave now?"

Derek tossed a grin over his shoulder and picked something out of the shorts' pocket.

Condom. Good man.

She watched him walk back toward her, muscles bunching and releasing, utterly natural and unselfconsciously naked in this lovely place.

Come to think of it, she felt the same. Not worried he might find her flawed, not comparing her body to anyone else's. Her brain knew he wanted her. Her heart knew he wanted her just the way she was.

Come on, Addie, you're romanticizing him the same way you were romanticizing Kevin.

Maybe. But with Derek it wasn't so much a thinking process as an instinct.

He came up close, arms around her waist, and leaned back to examine her face. "I take it you changed your mind."

"Apparently." She tried to make eye contact, but the depth of his gaze was too intense, made her insides shuddery and sweet, so she contented herself with gazing at his chin, his shoulders, his chest, only chancing a glance up at him now and then, as much as she could take.

"You're sure?"

"Very." She traced the line of his collarbone with her finger. "How did you find me here?"

"Sarah."

Addie's finger stopped at his sternum. Her mouth dropped open. "*Sarah* told *you* I was here?"

Why hadn't she sent Kevin?

"Yeah." Derek nodded, looking unexpectedly wary. "Right after she found out Kevin spent last night with Carrie."

"Kevin—" Addie's mouth dropped wider. "He—"

"I'm sorry, Addie."

She stared at him, trying to process all this, waiting for the pain, the rage, the feeling of betrayal. That rat Kevin. Not wanting to let her in his room. All that crap about wanting to get to know her before they slept together. The funny high-voiced whimper she heard....

Addie burst out laughing. What an idiot she'd been.

Derek blinked in surprise. "You think that's funny?"

Addie shrugged. "Parts of it are. The whole night was practically farcical. Me with you by mistake, then bumping into Kevin who had another woman with him the whole time. And it's funny in a sort of sad way how hard I worked not to see Kevin as he is. And it's funny in a

FREE Merchandise is 'in the Cards' for you!

Dear Reader,

We're giving away FREE MERCHANDISE!

Seriously, we'd like to reward you for reading this novel by giving you **FREE MERCHANDISE** worth over $20. And no purchase is necessary!

You see the Jack of Hearts sticker above? Paste that sticker in the box on the Free Merchandise Voucher inside. Return the Voucher promptly...and we'll send you valuable Free Merchandise!

Thanks again for reading one of our novels—and enjoy your Free Merchandise with our compliments!

Pam Powers

Pam Powers

P.S. Look inside to see what Free Merchandise is **"in the cards"** for you!

HB-FM-08/13

We'd like to send you two free books to introduce you to the Harlequin® Blaze™ series. These books are worth over $10, but they are yours to keep absolutely FREE! We'll even send you 2 wonderful surprise gifts. You can't lose!

REMEMBER: Your Free Merchandise, consisting of **2 Free Books** and **2 Free Gifts**, is worth over $20.00! No purchase is necessary, so please send for your Free Merchandise today.

Plus TWO FREE GIFTS!

We'll also send you two wonderful FREE GIFTS (worth about $10), in addition to your 2 Free Harlequin Blaze books!

YOUR FREE MERCHANDISE INCLUDES...

2 FREE Harlequin® Blaze™ Books
AND 2 FREE Mystery Gifts

FREE MERCHANDISE VOUCHER

2 FREE BOOKS and **2 FREE GIFTS**

Please send my Free Merchandise, consisting of
2 Free Books and **2 Free Mystery Gifts**.
I understand that I am under no obligation to buy
anything, as explained on the back of this card.

150/350 HDL F42D

Please Print

FIRST NAME

LAST NAME

ADDRESS

APT.#   CITY

STATE/PROV.   ZIP/POSTAL CODE

NO PURCHASE NECESSARY!

▲ Detach card and mail today. No stamp needed. ▲

HB-FM-08/13 · © 2013 HARLEQUIN ENTERPRISES LIMITED. ® and ™ are trademarks owned and used by the trademark owner and/or its licensee. Printed in the U.S.A.

sweet way that Sarah relinquished her need to attack you long enough to let me try."

"Mmm." His eyes warmed. "I like the way you attack me."

"After Kevin…well, you're not exactly a booby prize."

"No." His eyes dropped appreciatively below her neck. "I get that one."

"Aw, jeez." Addie pretended disgust at his pun, disgust which crumbled when he darted forward and fixed his mouth onto her breast.

Mmm. She let her head fall back, concentrating on the wet heat of his tongue and lips tugging her nipple, sending pleasure signals traveling through her body down between her legs.

"Make love to me, Derek." She dropped slowly to her knees, pulling him with her—not that he resisted.

"I definitely plan to," he whispered. "I wanted to from the moment you said hello on the front steps of the house."

"Me, too." She held out her arms for him. Their words were strictly carnal, but somehow Addie felt as if they were speaking from the heart. Even though they were in this for only a few days, it didn't feel like a hit-and-run relationship. It felt much richer, more important to each of them.

Oh, please, Addie, you're getting laid, stop trying to make it into something more.

Telling the critical pain-in-the-butt voice in her head to shut up, Addie clasped Derek's warm, wide body to hers, reveling in its power, how small he made her feel, but how safe.

He paid her breasts more attention while he ran his hand up and down her belly, slightly lower with each stroke until he touched the top of her pubic curls, then lower and lower, making her gasp.

"You like that?"

"Oh, yes." She arched her hips up, inviting his hand to explore further, her arousal building again to a fever pitch. *"Yes."*

"I like it, too, Addie." He lifted his head to gaze at her while one finger traveled slowly over her pubic bone, nudging her clitoris, stroking over it, making the slide down between her labia.

Addie whimpered, eyes cemented to his, helpless under his touch. His finger dipped inside her. She gasped at the intrusion, hungry between her legs as she'd never been before. Derek withdrew his finger and painted it, slippery wet, over her clitoris, warming where the sun's weight already lay.

Addie nearly came right there, had to breathe and back down. She wanted him inside her. She wanted him coming with her.

Again, his finger slid and thrusted and painted. Again she fought the orgasm, trembling in his arms, her breath a series of stuttering gasps. Again, and again he brought her to the edge, until she was ready to scream.

"I can't do this much longer," she whispered. "I want you."

He pulled on the condom, spread her legs wide and knelt between them, making her feel open and vulnerable to him, breeze blowing intimately on her sex. His eyes traveled her body, rested on her face.

"You're beautiful, Addie."

He made her feel beautiful. Inside and out. Nothing else mattered right now. "Come to me, Derek. Please."

He walked forward on his hands, his body held over hers. Addie lifted her head and they both looked down. At her—wide-open. At him—hard and ready.

Then he lowered himself, only halfway. Addie reached

for his erection, impatient to guide it where she wanted it so badly.

"Addie."

"Yes." She was breathless with anticipation. Why was he holding back?

"Look at me."

She met his eyes and he pushed inside her, slowly, an inch, back out, then farther, stretching her, filling her. She closed her eyes—the connection and emotions were too intense—and let herself concentrate only on the animal, on the thrust of him way inside her, friction slow and steady in spite of how wet she was. The weight of him on top of her, the clean just-showered smell of his skin. The way he moved leisurely in and out, showing no impatience. She didn't want him to hurry. They had the beach to themselves and the rest of the afternoon.

For a while, his rhythm went on unchanged, as they got to know each other's sounds and movements, exploring textures and shapes.

Then Derek pulled almost all the way out, made love to her with only the first inch or two of his penis, causing a light tug on her clitoris, just enough to make her crazy but not quite enough stimulation to come.

Torture. She moaned involuntarily, began breathing harshly, nearly panting. She had to come *now*.

When she was about to put her hand down and take care of it herself, Derek thrust all the way in and began an earnest, powerful drive.

Addie gave a yell, more noise than she'd ever made during lovemaking, but she was no longer in control of her body or herself. The orgasm was coming so slow and hot and hard, she wasn't even sure she'd survive it.

Just before its peak, she opened her eyes in surrender and locked on to Derek's.

"Yes," he whispered. Somehow he knew. How did he know? "Let go, come for me."

Gripping his shoulders, bracing herself, Addie yelled again, lost in the explosion of pleasure, and the doubling of its intensity as she realized he was coming with her, inside her, pulsing as she contracted over and over until the waves of pleasure subsided, leaving them locked together, breaths heaving.

When she could speak again, Addie stroked the dark head resting on her breast. "That was wonderful, Derek."

"Mrhgm."

She giggled. "You're welcome."

He lifted his head unsteadily and blinked down at her. "Are we still alive?"

"I...think so."

"My God, Addie." He was smiling, but she heard the awe in his voice and saw it in his eyes. "That was... I'm kind of glad you changed your mind."

"I'm kind of glad Sarah told you where I was."

"And that Kevin got laid last night."

"And that I found your room by mistake."

He kissed her then, long slow kisses that instead of heating up her body, heated up her heart.

Uh-oh.

See? You can't handle casual sex. You are not a wild woman. What made you think you could?

She kissed him back, only letting herself enjoy the smooth masculine feel of his mouth against hers, her hands stroking the long muscles in his back, sweeping up to his powerful shoulders.

He pulled out reluctantly, removed the condom and lay facing her on the towel. For a while they were quiet, gazing into each other's eyes. She didn't find it hard to do anymore. He seemed almost familiar; there was some part of his gaze that now jumped out and included her. It was not the way she'd ever imagined looking at someone she barely knew. There was no fear, not even of judgment. This was so new. So different.

And she'd have to say goodbye to him in only two days.

"You know what?" She stroked the side of his face, unable to stop wanting to feel his skin under her fingers. "That's the most spontaneous thing I've ever done."

He turned to kiss her palm. "It certainly got my attention."

"I'm not usually like that."

"You don't generally flaunt your very beautiful naked body in front of men you don't know very well? I'd say that's a good thing."

She laughed. "I mean…I didn't think that was something I would do. Or even could do."

He turned her gently onto her back and lay half over her. "Maybe it's the Maine air."

"Maybe it's some mind-altering drug Paul and Ellen put in breakfast."

"Maybe you were possessed by aliens."

"Maybe I feel safe with you." She wrinkled her nose. "Nah, that's ridiculous."

That deep chuckle again. Addie wanted to bottle it and bring it home with her. They had two more days and she already missed it.

"I hope you do, because you are safe with me. As for not being spontaneous, we all have busy lives, duties, things we need to accomplish every day. Spontaneity is a luxury. You're on vacation now, you can afford it."

"True." She frowned thoughtfully, outlining his lips with her pinky. They were beautiful lips. Of course right then she was so infatuated, she'd probably think he had beautiful toenails. "But I do tend to be uncomfortable with anything not planned ahead."

"Maybe you'll embrace the dark side a little more now." He kissed one cheek, her other cheek, her nose, her forehead. "It's not as if you have to strip for every guy you meet for the rest of your life. Try new things, see how they feel. Baby steps."

Addie stroked the hard curve of his shoulder. It meant a lot that he took her neuroses so calmly and seriously. "You feel really good, Derek."

"So do you, Addie."

They smiled at each other. Incredible happiness and incredible peace, an amazing combination. "Tell me something."

"Mmm?"

"No, I mean tell me something. Anything. Everything." She grinned at the alarm on his face. "Tell me about your childhood."

"Ah." He rolled onto his back, lips curved in a wistful smile. "My childhood was a study in conflict. Between me, the boy who'd wanted a life on the sea since he was old enough to read *Kidnapped,* and my parents, who'd planned for me to go to business school like my dad and brothers ever since I was born."

"Ah, the family black sheep!"

"Baaa."

She propped herself up so she could see his face. "Tell me more."

"Let's see. I worked crap jobs on boats in Boston Harbor till I was old enough to leave home. Then I got crap jobs on boats in Miami until I went to school, graduated and worked my way up, saving every penny. At what I felt was the right time, I let everyone know I was looking for the right boat. And then one day I heard about her."

"Love at first sight?"

"You have no idea."

Oh, great, she was jealous of a boat. "Picture in your wallet?"

"Nope." He half lifted his head to peer at her. "I should have one, huh?"

"Absolutely." She stroked the firm, rounded planes of his chest. "I'd love to see her."

"Who knows what life will bring. Maybe you will someday."

"Maybe." She paid close attention to his body, not wanting to look at him. The topic was too charged to be under discussion this soon. "So you met the love of your life…."

"I had some money set aside by my grandparents, and landed a loan with help from a guy I worked for as first mate for years."

"He didn't mind you were leaving?"

"He knew he had no choice." Derek adjusted his head on the towel, expression fiercely proud. "He was a good guy. I enjoyed working for him. But I wanted to be boss. It's in my blood I guess. All Bates boys are bossy."

She loved the idea of him working hard, making his dream come true all by himself, becoming captain and owner of his own little kingdom. It was kind of a turn-on. But then calling something about Derek a turn-on was sort of like saying the sun was warm.

"It's amazing what you've done. I admire you."

"Oh." He looked embarrassed, but in a way that told her he was pleased by her compliment. "Thanks."

"It took courage and determination."

"Hmm." He sat up and squeezed her hand. "I think it was just what I wanted to do, so I did it."

"But a lot of people don't get to do what they want. Or can't. Or are afraid to."

"Yeah?" He studied her chin then planted a kiss in the perfect spot. "What would you do if you could?"

"Oh." She cast her mind around, mortified not to come up with anything thrilling. Maybe she should invent something—skydiving or hiking Mount Everest. But when she looked into Derek's serious brown eyes she couldn't tell him a lie. Even a little one. She wanted this to be real for the short time they had. "I'm pretty contented, actually."

"Hey, a lot of people can't do that, either. So you're just as remarkable."

Addie rolled her eyes. "Nice try."

He laughed and kissed her everywhere he could reach, teasing playful kisses that made her squeal and giggle like a silly schoolgirl.

Except she didn't feel silly. She felt…fabulous.

"What do you say we go rinse off, Addie?"

Addie pretended to shudder. "In that water?"

"In our private pool." He stood and held out his hand. "Which happens to be filled with that water, yeah."

"Tell you what." Addie was already getting to her feet. "You go, I'm outta here."

She took off toward the path. He caught up to her in about three strides and snagged her around the waist. "Oops. Ocean's the other way."

"Help, help! *Torture!*" The word ended in a squeal as he picked her up and ran with her to the water. "So help me, Derek, if you dump me into that freezing—"

Of course he did. She found her feet, and lunged up, flung her arms around his neck and knocked him off balance so he fell in, too.

There. They were even. With a shout, he rocketed up out of the water as fast as she had, grabbed her hand and pulled her back out onto the shore and back to his towel where they sat absorbing the sun's warmth, bodies glowing from the cold, lungs working to overcome the shock.

Addie had never had this much fun with a lover. Her first serious boyfriend, Todd, had been intense and bookish, a lovely sweet guy. Her second, Leo, had been a little sunnier maybe, but neither were the type who liked to play like this.

Addie apparently liked men who played. As long as they respected her in the morning.

"I suppose we should think about going back?" The minute she spoke, she regretted it. Practical, sensible Addie. Had she always been such a spoilsport?

"Yes, we should." He frowned hard then his face cleared. "There, we thought about it."

Addie burst into giggles. She was enjoying herself a ridiculous amount. And if he wanted to stay, then he must be feeling the same. "That's settled, then?"

"At least until we get hungry."

"Gosh. Now that you mention it…" She blinked at him sweetly, reclined onto her elbows and let her knees open slowly all the way to flat. "I'm getting *hungry* right now."

"Addie Sewell. Beautiful, funny *and* a nymphomaniac." He waggled his eyebrows and adopted a lounge lizard accent. "*Now* how much would you pay?"

"Oh, that is just *nasty*." She pretended to struggle away from him, letting herself be overpowered of course. He grinned wickedly, then turned one-eighty and positioned himself with his hands on either side of her hips, his knees to one side of her head, his face…lowering.

Addie lay back blissfully, desire responding to his skill, noticing deeper intimacy with him this time, not only from their already having explored each other's bodies, but from the joy of letting loose and being silly and child-like together. Two different kinds of vulnerability, both bringing them closer together.

She could fall for this guy.

Yes, yes, she knew it was too soon, way too soon. But everything about being with him felt so different from any relationship she'd—

Ooh. His fingers had joined his tongue. He was spoiling her. She reached over and pulled at his leg, wanting him to feel this good, too.

Derek understood, moving to kneel astride her head. Addie guided his penis into her mouth; he tasted clean and salty from the sea. She tried to vary the speed and pressure of her lips, listening to his breath hissing when she hit a rhythm or spot he really liked, but what he was doing to her at the same time made it very hard to focus on anything but her gathering frenzy for him.

Just when she was about to cry uncle, Derek pulled back, flicking gently with his tongue, then lowered his mouth and sucked firmly, pushing two fingers deep inside her.

She was lost. Her orgasm hit fast and intense from the beginning. Barely keeping herself under control, she fingered the shaft of Derek's cock, keeping the rhythm going with her mouth at his tip, then reached under and past his balls to the hidden root of his penis.

He inhaled sharply, moaned and seconds later erupted, his muscles contracting, making the sexiest sounds of ecstasy she'd ever heard.

Oh, my.

She lay, blissful, panting, heart swollen and aching with all she felt. What they'd done was nothing she'd ever consider a loving or sweet act, and yet…that's exactly how it had felt with him, each giving to the other. Derek turned around shakily and collapsed next to her, pulling her to him, cradling her head on his chest, nearly bringing tears to her eyes with his tenderness. The breeze had picked up, blowing cooler sweet air over them. The tide was coming in, waves rolling lazily toward them over the warm sand.

This was paradise.

"Addie." He took her face in his hands. "You are incredible."

Then he kissed her, differently from the way he'd kissed her before. Gently, reverently, over and over. Her heart swelled larger, dangerously so, that intense sweet ache in her chest told her she was in serious trouble over this man.

Could she fall for him?

Yes. That worry had been there since the night they watched the sunset together, Addie just hadn't been able to admit it to herself.

After today, however, she had a brand-new worry. Not whether she'd fall for Derek Bates, but how far she already had.

10

"Are you hungry? For food this time?" Derek drew his hand down Addie's firm stomach, over her pelvis, fingers brushing lightly through her curls. He could touch this woman all day long. In fact, he intended to.

"Actually, yes." She turned to him, face rosy and bright. "I've been in denial, though, because I'm enjoying this so much I don't want to go back up to the house."

"What would you say if you found out I have a cooler up in the woods packed with lunch?"

"Hmm." She bunched her mouth, thinking it over. "I guess I'd have to say you're the world's most perfect man."

Derek laughed and got to his feet. "That'll do."

He climbed the small rise into the woods, heading toward the spot where he'd left the cooler. Around Addie he felt more natural and relaxed than any woman he could remember being with. Something about her made him feel he didn't have to hide any part of himself. He'd been playing a role so often on board *Joie de Vivre* that he'd apparently made it a habit to turn his real self off, turn on the charm and say only safe and appropriate things, acting with professional decorum at all times—even onshore to a certain extent—so that his clean and sober reputation stayed intact.

Something else was surfacing now, too, from deep in his subconscious, rising slowly, about to break through. He'd noticed it first around Paul and Ellen, who were constantly connecting with a look, a touch, a murmured word or two. They had a future of that special linkage ahead of them, years and years, for the rest of their lives. Watching them had made Derek aware of how much time he spent alone, even among people.

He couldn't say he'd bonded deeply with anyone in his family, though of course he loved them all. At his first jobs at sea, he'd contented himself with "buddy" relationships with crew members, and there was always distance from his superiors—the same distance he kept now as captain. Paul had probably been his first substantive friendship. He'd had relationships now and then with women, but they'd always been secondary to his career, and never very consuming. With Addie, he felt truly connected.

He grabbed the cooler and jumped back down onto the warm sand, brought it over to her, feeling like a commoner proffering gifts to a queen.

No, that wasn't right. She never made him feel common. She made him feel like a man worth loving.

It would be easy to qualify his feelings for Addie, saying they must only be superficial, that he and she had only known each other such a short time, yadda yadda, all the common sense stuff. But deep in his soul, where there existed only truth, he was getting the beginnings of a message so huge he was afraid of hearing it, afraid of dwelling on it, not sure if he was afraid it was true or afraid that it wasn't.

Addie was The One.

Crazy talk. He was way, way ahead of himself.

"Here we go." He plunked the cooler onto the sand and arranged the towel so they could sit together facing the water, then opened the lid. *"Les sandwiches du jambon."*

"Good Lord, what have you made for me?"

"Ham sandwiches."

Addie giggled. "So chic, Pierre."

"Ain't it?" He unwrapped a sandwich he'd made when he stopped into the main house for a lightning fast shower after chopping all that wood, and for condoms. It had occurred to him if his plan for Addie's morning worked out he'd want to spend a lot of private time with her that afternoon as well, so lunch was a good idea. Paul and Ellen had nothing planned for the group until the rehearsal dinner that night. Many of the guests had decided to spend the afternoon on the mainland. They were free and clear until early evening.

"Thank you. It looks delicious." She took the thick sandwich—of ham, cheese and cucumber slices on whole wheat bread, and a can of lemon-flavored sparkling water.

They ate for a while in comfortable silence, then Derek started smiling—he couldn't help it. Addie had that adorable frown across her forehead, which he was starting to learn meant she was working something out in her mind.

"It's funny," she said eventually. "I almost didn't want to come to this wedding."

"Yeah?" A tiny shock jolted his chest, as if he was suffering the idea of never having met her. For crying out loud. She *did* come.

"Anything that promised to take me out of my comfortable everyday routine felt like a threat. It's kind of scary to look back now and see how stuck I was. I hope I never go back to that."

"You won't if you don't want to. And for the record, I'm very glad you came." Understatement of the millennium. She'd already changed his life. From now on he wouldn't settle for less than this remarkable level of affinity and of intimacy.

"Me, too." She smiled at him, her dark eyes warm and a little shy, dimple sweet in her right cheek. His heart seemed to double in size, straining to get out of his chest. "Tell me more about your life as the big romantic yacht captain."

"Ha." He took a sip of water. "Nonstop fun and glamour."

"I knew it!"

"Let's see. Which would be more thrilling, talking about managing a hardworking, squabbling crew stuck in close quarters for weeks at a time, or discussing the hours spent charting courses and worrying about weather, or dealing with annoying entitled passengers, or managing the budget, or hey, I know, understanding the paperwork and health regulations required by different ports, rarely getting a day off…are you still awake?"

"Wow." She chewed solemnly on a bite of sandwich. "I guess every job has its downside, huh. You still love it, though."

"Most of the time, yeah."

"There must be some glamorous parts to it."

"There are." He chased a bite of sandwich with water, realizing he'd been starving and glad he'd packed lots of food. Not only had he worked his body plenty today, he'd also been through an emotional Tilt-A-Whirl. "I've anchored at some of the most gorgeous spots in the world. Seen places I never would have dreamed of if I'd stayed in Massachusetts with my family."

"Hmm." Addie took another bite. Derek was intrigued. Usually this was where women sighed and batted their eyes and said they'd give anything to be able to come along on a trip, that it sounded so romantic. But Addie sat still, that slight frown creasing her forehead.

"It must be a lonely life."

For about three seconds he sat, stunned and oddly moved. She was right. It was a lonely life. But not that many people—no one he'd met—had ever figured that out.

"It can be." His voice had gone husky. He cleared his throat.

"It's also not a life conducive to having a family or a home. Not in a traditional way anyway. So it must seem like there's no real solution to loneliness."

Derek took a last big bite of sandwich to delay answering. What was he going to say, *You're right. And quite honestly, I didn't even consider marriage and kids until I met you the day before yesterday?* It would be a great way to see her gorgeous rear—running away from him as fast as possible. He wouldn't blame her.

What was happening to him? His career, his boat, they'd been everything to him his whole life, first as a dream, then a reality.

"I think I'd have to meet the right woman." He wanted to roll his eyes at the cliché. "Well, obviously. I wouldn't want to be with the *wrong* one."

"No kidding." She gestured with her sandwich. "You need to find someone who'd be fine on her own all the time. Raising kids with no help whatsoever."

He did roll his eyes then. "Yeah, piece of cake, there are probably five or six on the planet."

They laughed together, though a part deep inside him felt vulnerable and pained, like they were poking fun at something too personal. "What about you, you want the traditional marriage?"

"I…" She stopped, looking pensive. "Funny, I was going to say yes, immediately, but you know, I'm starting to question a lot of stuff about myself this weekend. Maybe I need to think about it. I definitely don't want to be home alone raising kids, so…you know, just to spare you asking me."

More laughter, strained this time, no, not too funny. Painful and vulnerable times two. "Tell me more."

She tipped her head to one side, considering. "It's funny, having been here, seeing Kevin, meeting you— this week is about Paul and Ellen's wedding, but it's also feeling like a crossroads for me, as if I'm coming to a place in life where I can choose to be different going forward."

"Different how?"

"More adventurous. Taking more risks. Trying new things."

He nodded and took a bite of sandwich to hide his reaction, which was a fierce possessive need to drag her back to Hawaii and onto *Joie de Vivre* so she couldn't try this new wildness out on anyone else.

The power of the feeling shocked him. Maybe this was a crossroads for him, too. The idea of leaving here, the camaraderie, the community and Addie, and sailing off with his crew and a bunch of strangers—the life he'd chosen, the life he'd worked so hard to be able to live—it was not appealing the same way it always had.

"What would you do? Take up skydiving? Start a career as a stripper?"

"Ha!" She made a face. "Not likely. I'm still me."

"I like that about you."

"Mmm, thanks." She closed the space between them for a kiss. Maybe she intended it to be brief, but Derek had other ideas. Her mouth was warm and soft and tasted like lemon sparkling water. She was delicious. He cupped his hand around her head and held her close, kissing her until his desire started rising again. And by the whimper she gave, he knew the excitement was mutual.

What torture next week to be on his boat thinking about this woman and knowing he couldn't hold her again. The *Joie de Vivre* had always been his ultimate refuge, his sanctuary, his kingdom. This woman could change all that. He wasn't sure he liked her having that much power over him and his life. But he wasn't sure he had a choice.

"Tell me the wild things you'd like to do," he murmured.

"Hmm. Maybe I'll take ballet." She didn't resist when he took her plate and put it on the sand then returned to kissing her, dragging her across his lap, wanting to keep her safely close to him. "I loved ballet when I was a girl. Maybe take that up again."

"Mmm, Addie in a tutu. I like the idea."

"Or maybe…" Her voice lowered and became slightly husky. She tipped her head to give him better access to the soft skin of her neck, tasting of salt, cocoa butter and Addie. "Maybe I'll take an online lit class."

Derek sucked in air, as if she was wildly arousing him. "A *lit* class. Addie I'm not sure how much more I can stand."

"And…" Addie sat up and put her hand to his chest, her gaze smoldering. She pushed until he was forced to lie back on the towel, then she straddled him on her hands and knees. "Maybe I'll learn French."

"Oh, la la." He growled and pulled her down to kiss him, molding her body on top of his. "Addie, I just want you to know that if you feel the need to try out anything different, you know, to bring out this wilder, primal, sex monster side of yourself, seriously, feel free. Right now. On top of me. I can take it. Really. I promise."

She was giggling madly, which made her wiggle just a

little, which was doing some truly great things for his man parts. Then her laughter subsided. She rested her head on his shoulder and went still. They lay there together, breathing in the clean sea air. A boat passed somewhere not too far off, engines throbbing, radio occasionally crackling to life.

Addie lifted her head, hair spilling over her forehead, cheeks flushed, eyes sultry, lips parted. "You're on."

He lay there, hardly able to believe the change in her. His cock reacted, hardening nearly fully in record time. All she'd done was look at him.

"You need to put on another condom."

He said nothing, scrambled to obey, had it on and was lying back down within seconds.

She straddled him again, lifted herself to her knees, the strength in her thighs controlling the height of her hips.

Not low enough.

As if she heard him, she lowered herself until she was sitting at the base of his erection, pressing it against his abdomen. His cock felt nestled in the warmth of her sex. He knew more was coming. He couldn't wait.

Addie lifted her arms over her head, pulling her breasts up, lengthening her torso. Then she began to sway, sliding her sex over him, stimulating his cock, undulating her body, eyes closed, like a belly dancer in a trance.

It was the sexiest thing Derek had ever seen, all the more so because he knew what she had to fight to be this free with him, because he knew this was a vote of confidence and trust in their intimacy and in him, that she felt comfortable and safe enough to let loose.

He groaned and grabbed her hips, pushing his up to increase the pressure, going from aroused to nearly desperate in a matter of a minute.

She caught his mood, began to ride him gently, rocking her hips up and back instead of side to side.

When he wasn't sure how much longer he could stand that, she pressed her hands into the sand on either side of his head and lifted, allowing his penis to come to full attention. Allowing him to feel the loss of warmth and the coolness of the breeze.

Only for a moment. Thank goodness.

Her hips lowered again, just to the tip of his cock, trapping it, then circling gently, making him use all his strength not to shove inside her, pump into her softness until he found release.

"I'm psychic, did you know that?"

"Nope." He spoke through clenched teeth.

"I am. And I'm getting something from you…" She gazed sightlessly off into the distance. "Wait… Yes, got it. You want to be inside me."

"Amazing." He sounded as if he was strangling.

"All the way."

"Yes. *Yes.*"

"Hmm." She came down farther. An inch of him disappeared. Her sex was warm and tight around the tip of his penis. He fisted his hands, swallowed convulsively.

"Do you like that, Derek?"

He nodded, sweat breaking out on his forehead, completely under her control, and not minding at all.

"How about this?" She moved lower; another inch of him slid inside her, another inch sensually enveloped. He wanted to pound his fists in the sand.

"Yes. I like that, too. More, please."

"Like this?" She hesitated, poised, making him wait. Then bore down powerfully and took him all the way in.

He gave a yell he was ashamed of then forgot his shame as she moved fiercely up and down. He tried to slow her movements, tried to stop her, somehow. But she was relentless, gripping his cock with her body, releasing and gripping again, panting in his ear, whispering what he felt like inside her, hot and hard and making her crazy with pleasure.

He was lost, too far over the edge to stop. With another shout he came so hard he felt as if his body was trying to turn inside out.

Oh, man.

"Addie." He could barely say her name.

"Mmm?" Her eyes were bright with triumphant pleasure. He'd never seen anything so beautiful.

He had to catch his breath, pulling her down to clasp her in his arms. "I want you to understand something."

"Yes?"

"It is physically impossible for me to come three times in this short a time."

"Really." He could hear the smile in her voice.

"I think you must be a witch. Or a shape-shifter."

"Supernatural sex." She kissed his neck contentedly. "Cool."

"Except for one thing."

"What's that?"

"You didn't get your third."

"Oh, no." She lifted her head. "I can't come that many times, either. Seriously, that was wonderful just like that."

"Uh-huh." He was already traveling down between her legs, aching to taste her.

"No, Derek, I really don't think I…*oh.*"

He'd gone to work, loving her taste, the supple give of her sex, the way she writhed under his tongue and his fingers.

"Maybe…" She stopped for a gasp as he changed his rhythm. "Maybe *one* more."

When she came apart, minutes later, moaning and gripping his arms, he felt her pleasure and satisfaction as if he'd come again himself.

He was falling for her. How could this happen so fast and so intensely? It made no sense…went against everything he thought he believed about love and about caution and about common sense.

Worse, and far more foolish, the idle fantasy of taking her out on his boat to live with him instead of returning her to the city had begun to change into the beginnings of a serious idea.

11

PAUL AND ELLEN'S rehearsal dinner was ending. The last lobster had been ravenously consumed, rolls and salad demolished, blueberry, raspberry and chocolate cream pies decimated. The group was lolling around the bonfire on the beach where they'd eaten, chatting while they finished off the keg. This was to be their last night on Storness Island. The next day, Saturday, they'd spend the morning cleaning and packing, then the trip back to the mainland for Paul and Ellen's late afternoon wedding and reception at the beautiful house in Machias owned by the Bossons' close friends, the Brisbanes. Sunday they'd all go home.

Sarah sat watching the flames, full of lobster, pie and confusion, nursing a last beer. She hadn't had many— this was her third in three or four hours. She wasn't in the mood for drinking. Most of the evening she'd smiled and chatted and acted the part of the happy groom's sister— which she was, no question, very happy for Paul and for Ellen, whom she adored. But the reason for her uncharacteristically somber mood eluded her, and therefore its solution was similarly out of reach.

Every time she felt some understanding approaching she'd do everything in her power to go inside herself and grab it—but always at that instant whatever she was after, whatever part she'd managed to comprehend, disintegrated again into confusion.

In other words, something was massively bugging her and she was effing clueless as to what to do about it.

This was not like her. She'd always thought of herself as sunny and optimistic, knowing what she wanted and how to go about getting it—as long as it wasn't a man. This weekend had dislodged her from that certainty, and tossed her into a who-am-I? abyss.

She hated that.

One of the guys Paul worked with, Evan she thought his name was, stood up on the other side of the bonfire and hoisted his cup of beer. "Thought I'd say a few things about the bride and groom taking the big plunge tomorrow."

Murmurs of encouragement came from around the fire. Evan went on to talk about his friendship with Paul, and told a funny story from Paul and Ellen's early years dating, when Paul bought her the world's most hideous sweater which Ellen pretended to like and still wore.

Sarah smiled at the couple, her heart contracting with a wistful pain. Envious? Yes. Their faces were glowing; they were constantly touching each other. It was sickening.

Sarah had wondered for a lot of years whether Paul was in love with Addie. She'd never asked, because she was so afraid the answer would be yes, and then she'd have to cope with an impossible situation since she knew Addie had never noticed Paul as anything but a buddy. Around Addie, Paul had either been quiet and worshipful, eager to please, or trying too hard to be cooler than he was.

After he started dating Ellen, he'd become steady and mature, yet also able to be entirely and proudly his goofy charming self. No posturing, no going quiet, no puppy-dogging. This was the real deal.

Imagine, being accepted so entirely in love that you didn't have to hide any of yourself, didn't constantly have to fear judgment and rejection. To relax so completely into someone that you might even discover parts of yourself you didn't know were there. Paul had found his inner alpha and had stepped up to the plate for his family, for Ellen's family and for their friends on many occasions, where before he might have wanted to, but ultimately have talked himself out of the risk.

How ironic, to have to feel safe enough in yourself before you could take any risks, when finding the person who could help you feel that safe took the biggest risk of all—making yourself completely open and vulnerable to someone else.

Would Sarah ever find that safety? Not if she kept falling in love with the men who'd risk nothing.

Evan finished and sat down. Another friend rose, a girlfriend of Ellen's. She talked about how cynical Ellen had gotten about men and about dating, so that for the first six weeks of her relationship with Paul, she kept saying he had to be some kind of total pervert or criminal because no one could be that wonderful. Of course her friends saw through this, and knew she was mentally shopping for a wedding dress after their second date.

Sarah sighed. More of the irony of love. Finally finding someone perfect for you and not being able to accept that lightning had struck, because so much of dating was wading through utter crap. She could vouch for that. She'd be suspicious, too, after all she'd been through, if something so great was simply handed to her.

"Hi." Joe's whisper made her automatically shift to make room next to her, still mulling over the mysteries of love and life, still not sure what to conclude when it came to her own situation. He sat and casually extended his arm behind her back, leaning on his hands, listening attentively with her to Ellen's friend, then to a few others who stood and told stories—funny stories, sweet stories, poignant stories, all demonstrating what a good match Ellen and Paul made. After a few minutes, Sarah leaned into Joe, enjoying the moment and his arm behind her, feeling a little more relaxed now, and steadier. Joe did that to her.

The last toast finished, Paul and Ellen stood up to say good-night. They'd be spending the night separately as tradition dictated. Ellen would stay in their bedroom in the house, and Paul would bunk in Kevin's room.

Poor Carrie. Sarah snickered. Yes, she was glad the little you-know-what wasn't after Joe anymore. Joe deserved a lot better. But it was pretty disgusting that she'd gone so obviously after him and then jumped into bed with Kevin the second the opportunity presented itself. What was up with that? Pathetic if you asked Sarah. Which no one had.

Around them, people were standing, stretching, forming new groups or heading off into the woods toward the house or to their tents. Sarah wasn't ready to go to bed. She knew she wouldn't sleep with this dryer load of unidentifiable emotions tumbling inside her.

"Hey." She turned to Joe, who seemed nearly as moody and distracted as she felt. "Want to take a walk?"

"Sure." He stood and held out a hand to haul her to her feet. "Which way?"

Sarah shrugged. "Doesn't matter. How about sunset point?"

"Okay."

They stopped at the house to get flashlights and a couple of old quilts to wrap up in since the night promised to be chilly. Fall came early to Maine, and late August nights could offer a pretty convincing taste of September.

They made their way down the cranberry covered hill to the prominent outcropping where they spread one quilt on the soft ground above the ledge and huddled under the other, flashlights off, staring out over the dark water.

"Nice rehearsal dinner."

"It was great." He yawned.

"Tired?"

"Yeah. We introvert types get worn out by all this fun."

She laughed. "Poor Joe, all those annoying good times."

"Uh-huh." He nudged her affectionately with his shoulder. "I'm not sure how I survived enjoying myself."

"Well, it's almost over."

He was silent so long she turned to look at him. "Joe?"

"Sorry, what?"

"Hello?" She'd obviously startled him out of some deep thought. He wasn't generally the brooding type. "I said the week is almost over."

"Yeah, I know."

Sarah frowned. Something was bothering him, too. "Guess we go back to the old routine, huh. You at your job, me at mine, seeing each other once in a while."

"Could be."

"We could make a pledge absolutely to have dinner once a week. At that Thai place you like down near Symphony Hall."

"Maybe."

Maybe? Really? Okay, this was serious. "What's the matter, Joe?"

"Me? Nothing."

"Come on." She nudged him with her shoulder, too, but hard, punishing him. "This is me you're talking to.

What's going on? Is it Carrie? Are you devastated having lost her to Kevin?"

He snorted and sent her a look she didn't need to see clearly to know was toxic. "Please."

"Sorry."

"No, you're not."

"You're right. I'm not." Her voice came out harder than she expected. "If you'd gone for her I would have had to sock her. Or you. Or both."

"Sarah…"

Her stomach turned over. She knew that tone, one he almost never used. Last time was when his mom had been diagnosed with late stage cancer. "Yes, Joe."

"I've been offered a job in Phoenix."

"What?"

"You heard me," he said calmly.

Yes. She had. And she felt as if she'd been given that sock in the gut she was saving for Carrie.

Joe had been looking for a job without telling her. He'd gotten a job without telling her. He was going to move… and was telling her.

"Wow." Sarah swallowed convulsively. She'd need to try harder to sound pleased for him. "That's great, Joe."

"Thanks."

"You're welcome!" Ugh. Now she sounded perky. Her face was heating; there was a weird rushing sound in her ears, but she sounded like Miss America on speed. Or Carrie. "What will you be doing?"

"More of the same. Computer geeks are pretty indispensable. But I like the culture of the new place a lot. And it's more money, a good move up."

"Great!" Now she sounded manic. Very close to insane. She could not process this, could only keep asking the expected questions, trolling for basic information, when all she wanted to do was ask how in hell he could do this to her. "When did you hear?"

"They called me a few hours ago."

"Well…wow." She tried desperately to sound happy. She would not make this about her. If this was what he wanted, this was what he should have. Phoenix. Jeez. Wasn't that on the other side of the planet? "This is thrilling."

"Yeah."

Sarah forced a laugh. "You don't sound very thrilled, Joe."

"You don't, either."

No. She'd tried. But she couldn't bullshit Joe. Never had been able to. Maybe she needed to stop bullshitting everyone, and then the Joes of the world would find her.

Not damn likely.

She summoned all her strength, while her heart felt as if it were going to explode. Not have Joe around? Not see Joe? Be far away from Joe? She couldn't get her brain to comprehend a change that huge. Boston wouldn't be the same. "Trust me, I am incredibly happy for you. You deserve this. When do you start?"

"I haven't accepted the offer yet."

Hope. Giant shimmering globs of it, surrounding her like a bubble bath gone wrong.

"But you will?" The end of her sentence quavered, betraying her hope. She hadn't meant it to be a question. She hadn't meant to show her vulnerability.

"I'd be a fool to turn it down."

"You would." She nodded vigorously, voice too high and too loud. "You absolutely would. And you're not a fool."

He laughed bitterly. She'd never heard him sound like

that, and it frightened her. "I've been a fool for a long time."

"What's that supposed to mean?"

"Sarah…one of the reasons I applied for this job, was because I was starting to realize that I need to get on with my life. Career-wise, but also…I'd like to get married someday. And hanging around you so much, I realized was a way to avoid finding a woman I could really be with."

Sarah forced her eyes open as wide as possible, blinking rapidly. Joe in love. Joe married. Joe at home with babies and a wife.

Joe with a woman who wasn't Sarah.

Of course. Of course he deserved that. Of *course* he did. And she was going to be freaking crazy happy for him. Her new mantra: the world was not about her. She was done being Selfish Sarah. No one on earth had suffered more from that selfishness than Joe.

"Thank you for telling me." Her voice cracked. "I completely understand."

"Sarah." He turned to her, put his arms around her and drew her down so they were lying together under the quilt, fresh Maine air cooling their faces, waves gurgling and tumbling down under the cliff.

She burrowed against him, trying to relax, forcing her breathing as steady as she could manage, and feeling as if someone had just hollowed her out with a giant drill.

"I'll miss you, Sarah."

"Stop." She spoke sharply then made herself giggle as if it was all a big joke.

Her panic rose. This was no joke. She had to get out of there. She couldn't lie next to him anymore and pretend. She was going to cry, she was going to scream, she was going to throw up. This pain, this dread, it was all her fault.

"You'll be busy, Joe, you'll have a new city to get to know, a new...everything." A smiling blonde with Joe's babies, Joe's arm around her, Joe's mouth on hers. Joe, the man she would depend on for love, support, friendship— everything Sarah had been greedily lapping up for the last near-decade, giving nothing in return.

She threw off the quilt and stood. Nausea threatened. She ran from him, behind a clump of alders and fell to her knees, breathing deeply.

"Sarah! What happened? What's the matter?" He spoke sharply from worry. He'd cared about her so deeply for so long and she'd taken it all for granted.

The cool air slowly settled her stomach. She collapsed back onto her bottom on the mossy ground.

"Just...too much beer. I thought I was going to lose it. I'm fine. Really."

"Sure?"

"I should get to bed." Where she could fall apart in earnest. "Thanks for telling me your news. And congratulations, Joe. I'm proud of you."

"I'll walk you to the house."

Of course he would. If she'd thrown up he would have stood behind her and stroked her back, held her hair out of the way. He'd do that for his wife, for his kids, always steady, always reliable.

A real man.

She let him help her up, waited while he gathered the quilts, let him take her arm and guide her back, lighting the way with her flashlight.

Inside the house, a few who'd deserted the beach fire had built another one in the fireplace, sipping something from steaming mugs and chatting or reading.

At her bedroom door, Sarah smiled gratefully at Joe and gave him a quick hug, sickened by the irony of having realized how much he meant to her now that she was losing him. What a cliché. She felt utterly stupid and defeated.

In her room alone, she changed into her pajamas, used the bathroom and crawled into bed, not even trying to sleep, just letting the misery and pain wash over her, quietly bearing it, knowing this was what she deserved.

She could try to stop him. She could plead with him, beg him to stay, promise things would be different. But she wouldn't. She had no right to sabotage his happiness. And she was too confused right now to be sure of what she could offer him, and what she could realistically promise.

Sarah groaned and pulled the covers over her head. This maturity stuff was the absolute freaking *pits*. She wanted to cry, but if she cried she'd look like hell for her brother's wedding, and worry everyone, so she couldn't even do that.

Hours later, or not, she had no idea how long, Addie came in. Sarah pretended to be asleep, turned toward the wall, clutching the covers under her chin, breathing slowly and a little too loudly. She couldn't talk to anyone, even though Addie might need an ear or a shoulder. She and Derek must have had a hell of a morning and afternoon. They'd shown up just as the rehearsal dinner started, looking blissfully stunned. Sarah would ask tomorrow, listen tomorrow. Do what she could to advise. Not right now. She hadn't become that selfless.

Hours later—or not, she *still* had no idea how long— Addie's breathing slipped into its own slow, regular pattern, only Addie probably had no reason to fake being asleep. Sarah lay still awhile longer then threw off the covers. This was torture. She couldn't lie here anymore or she'd go stark raving nuts.

Tiptoeing across the pine floor, she unlatched the door

as quietly as she could and shut it behind her, hoping she hadn't disturbed Addie.

In the living room, watching the dying embers of the fire, sat Carrie.

Ew.

Sarah hesitated, not exactly jumping at the opportunity to share her insomnia with Carrie, then gave a quick wave and made a beeline for the bathroom, buying time to decide what to do. She could go outside, but it would feel cold and lonely out there. Back to bed wasn't an option, at least not yet. Maybe she could light a lamp and pretend to read something? Find another room in the house where she could sit? The kitchen?

In the end she decided to stay in the living room where it was warmest. Maybe Carrie wouldn't turn out to be such bad company. Or maybe she'd shut up.

"Mind if I join you?"

"Nope." Carrie lifted the blanket she'd been sitting under and offered half to Sarah.

The gesture reminded her of Joe, and brought on a fresh wave of pain. "Thanks, I'm fine."

"Insomnia a regular demon for you?" Carrie asked.

"Not usually." Sarah sat near the other end of the couch, hoping she could answer in monosyllables and then lapse into miserable silence and that Carrie would get the hint.

"It's my regular companion." Carrie got up and put another log on the fire. "My mom was the same way."

"Yeah?" Sarah wondered why Carrie wouldn't rather enjoy the warmth of Kevin, then she remembered Kevin and Paul were in the same room tonight. Ha.

"So if it's not a regular problem for you, what's up tonight?"

Sarah shrugged.

"Did y'all fight with Joe?"

Huh? Sarah stared at her. Joe couldn't have told her. He wouldn't.

"I saw you two together when I was coming back up from the beach. You both looked miserable. I thought maybe you were on the outs."

"We're just friends."

"Oh, I know *that*." She chuckled, making Sarah feel like an idiot for protesting against something Carrie hadn't implied. "Believe me, I know. Joe is totally the friend type."

Sarah bristled. She did not like this woman and she did not like the way she was talking about Joe. "What type is Kevin?"

"Kevin? He's a jerk."

Sarah blinked in surprise then snorted. "Good choice, then."

"I always go for jerks." She spoke as if she was talking about shopping for a type of shoe. "They're perfect when you don't want to get serious."

Sarah started feeling queasy again. "You go after jerks deliberately?"

"Well sure, honey."

"What about Joe?"

More of that annoying laugh. "I wasn't going after him. Just flirting. He seemed the type who needed to be flirted with."

Sarah made herself breathe. And unclench her fist. And not think any more about putting it into Carrie's face. "I'm sure he was grateful for whatever crumb you tossed him."

"I know, right?" Carrie completely missed Sarah's sarcasm.

"So why don't you want to get serious about anyone?"

"Are you kidding?" She gave an ugly guffaw. "Me?

Marriage? No, thank you, ma'am. I saw what it did to my mom. I'm steering clear of that slavery."

Sarah swallowed audibly. Her mother had described marriage the same way to a friend. Sarah had overheard her, and even though she'd been too young to understand, the tone of her mom's usually sweet voice had made the words stick in her head. "Well, then don't marry a jerk."

Carrie snorted. "They're all jerks. And if you make the mistake of thinking you found a good one, as soon as you fall for him, trust me, he turns jerk."

This was sounding familiar. Wheels started turning so hard in Sarah's brain, she would not be surprised if her scalp started steaming.

And then, there it was, what she'd been on the edge of figuring out all day. She was always falling for unavailable men and jerks, all along thinking what she wanted from them was a serious relationship. But, like Carrie, she was essentially making sure she'd never have one. The only difference was that Carrie knew that about herself and acted that way on purpose. Sarah had been ignoring her subconscious, acting on pure denial, moaning and bitching and playing the poor-me victim to whomever would listen.

But she'd just figured it out. And she knew she really had because now instead of waves of pain, she was getting a huge sense of relief, like her subconscious had been trying to tell her this for years and she resolutely ignored it, but now thank God she had finally paid attention.

Sarah was choosing the men deliberately out of fear. She was setting herself up to fail because she was afraid of taking that risk she'd been thinking about earlier, the risk of being that vulnerable.

That night on the beach with Joe, she'd wished on a falling star that she'd find someone to love who'd love her back. Joe had told her she couldn't see what was right under her nose. Tonight when she found out he was leaving Boston, her whole world threatened to collapse.

Oh, Joe.

She could totally see it now. See everything she'd been lucky enough to have for the last decade, and all she'd done was try to find it somewhere else.

Maybe…maybe if she hadn't screwed this up too badly, after the wedding she'd be able to show Joe exactly what she'd learned about men, and about relationships and most of all, about what this new Sarah wanted to try. With him.

12

DEREK THREW OFF the covers. What time was it, 1:00 a.m.? Two? He'd given up trying to sleep. What a messed up day. One of the most blissful afternoons he'd ever had, with a woman who affected him deeply, then during Paul and Ellen's really fun rehearsal dinner—lobsters that put every other one he'd eaten to shame boiled in a huge pot right on the beach—the whole afterglow aura had drifted away. He wasn't even sure when the downshift had started, or at what point he noticed. The evening started with warm glances between him and Addie and occasional surreptitious touches. By unspoken agreement, they both seemed to want to keep their new bond private.

As the evening drew on, as the partying intensified, as Paul and Ellen became more demonstrative, and the toasts longer and drunker and funnier and more poignant, the obvious hopelessness of his and Addie's situation had hit him. And it must have hit her, too, because her eyes had dulled, her smiles and cheers became as forced as his own. Not that he wasn't happy for Paul and Ellen, he couldn't be happier. Theirs was a strong and good relationship that would only grow stronger and better through marriage.

The problem? He and Addie had that potential, he could

feel it in his gut no matter how much his sensible side tried to explain it away with theories about animal attraction and infatuation, the fool's gold of love.

But there was no way they could make their happy-ever-after happen.

Part of what he loved about Addie was her strong and sensible side; she'd be a woman he could depend on to tackle life's decisions calmly. She'd never be a woman like Sarah, a maelstrom of impetuous and random choices. But that very characteristic meant she was unlikely to give up her life after a short affair and go trotting around the globe with him. Derek couldn't blame her. Neither was he willing to give up life aboard *Joie de Vivre* and stick himself into a suit and between four walls.

After dinner as the crowd dispersed, he'd taken Addie into a private place in the woods for a quick good-night. He'd kissed her, and they'd embraced fiercely. His body had responded to hers, he'd lowered his lips to her hair, inhaling her scent. She'd clung to him, pressing her face into his neck. Then they'd gone to bed, neither suggesting they do so together in his room. He wasn't sure of her reasons, but Derek knew his: if he got the chance to hold Addie in his arms all night, leaving her on Sunday would be that much more painful.

Now, body tortured by physical memories, and brain tortured by emotional ones, he was giving up the farce of trying to sleep and going downstairs. Maybe get a glass of milk or herbal tea or whatever he could find that might help him relax.

Though he had a feeling nothing would help get Addie out of his system.

He clumped downstairs with his flashlight and headed toward the glow emanating from the kitchen. Someone else up? Or had someone left a light on?

Joe was slumped over, face pressed against the wooden tabletop, a bottle of Irish whiskey by his head. Derek took two steps into the room and he sat up, squinting blearily to see who'd disturbed his beauty sleep, hair sticking up on one side, cheek and forehead red where they'd been resting on the table.

"Joe, man, what happened to you?"

Joe shook his head wearily. "Love."

"Love, huh." Derek opened the refrigerator, searching. Milk, water, lemonade, beer… He glanced back at the table. If they were going to be talking about love, maybe he needed whiskey, too. Though he'd get a bottle of water out for Joe. Looked like he could use a little dilution of the alcohol in his blood. "It's that bad?"

"It's worse."

"Uh-oh." Derek got a glass down from the cabinet and poured himself a couple of fingers of Jameson's, his favorite. Poor Joe. Something must have happened with Sarah. "Tell me about it."

Joe frowned. "Tell me about it like, 'yeah, I know what you mean,' or tell me about it, like really tell you about it?"

"Both." Derek lifted his glass in a toast. "You talk first."

"Mmph." Joe stretched and yawned, then hunched back over his whiskey. "I got my dream job offer today."

"Yeah? Congratulations." That clearly wasn't the bad news. Derek toasted Joe again and took a sip of whiskey. Its smooth burn coated his throat. Delicious. He should start stocking the stuff in his cabin for when he was there alone every night and needed anaesthetizing. "That's a very big deal."

"Thanks. The job is in Phoenix, which means I'd have to move."

"Ah." There was the problem. "Yeah, that'd be a helluva commute from Boston."

Joe acknowledged the joke with a bleak nod. "If I take it, then I have to say goodbye to Sarah. Which also means I'm saying goodbye to—"

"Don't tell me. Let me guess. All your hopes and all your dreams about a future with her." He laughed bitterly. Yeah, he sorta knew what that could feel like.

Joe looked bewildered. "How did you know?"

"I have my ways."

"Addie?"

Derek's turn to look surprised. "Uh…"

"Shit." Joe glowered at the table. "Just shit."

"Well put." Derek took another sip of whiskey. Looked like he and Joe had a lot in common right now. "So that's that with Sarah?"

"That's that."

No. Not after all they'd been through together. Derek couldn't accept that. He'd seen Sarah around Joe; she lit up like the moon. "She won't go with you?"

Joe laughed bitterly. "Oh, like *that* would happen."

"Did you ask her?"

"What, are you kidding me?" He laughed again, so painfully Derek had to hide a wince. "I think I've suffered enough humiliation tagging after her like a puppy for the past however many years."

"Hey, Joe. You love her."

Joe snorted, noticed his glass, picked it up and tossed back the tiny amount left. "The saddest part? I know exactly how long I've been her puppy. Nine years, eight months and four days since I met her at the Vassar bookstore in the checkout line. She'd cut in front of someone by mistake, and he was all bent out of shape. I stepped in and smoothed it over for her. We got talking. I fell for her in about five minutes."

"Does she know?"

"Of course she knows. *Everybody* knows." He flung out his arm and nearly knocked over the bottle, grabbed it at the last second, looked at it in surprise, then sloshed another finger into his glass. "Good old Joe, panting after Sarah while she goes after every guy she meets who's my most polar opposite. Including you."

Oof. Yeah. Derek would go back and erase that for Joe's sake if he could. "But look, none of those guys worked out. Including me. I never touched her by the way."

"Yeah, I know." He blew out a frustrated breath and let his head hang. "I'm not angry. It's not your fault you're incredibly good-looking and charming and exciting, or whatever else she needs that I'm not."

Derek contemplated the top of Joe's head, half feeling sorry for him, half wanting to tell him to grow a pair. "What do you think she needs?"

"The whole bad-boy shtick. That's not me." His head was nearly touching the table again. "It's never going to be me."

Derek leaned toward him, prodded him in the shoulder. "If Sarah really wanted that she would have stayed with at least one of these guys, right?"

"They all dumped her."

"Oh." This was not easy. Derek frowned, struggling to organize his thoughts. "Okay, here is my advice. If I was you, I'd start by telling her straight-out how you feel."

Joe's head lifted, eyes dull. He looked like hell. No way would Sarah go for him that way. "What if she tells me to get lost?"

"Dude, you're moving to Phoenix, how much more lost can you get?"

Joe nodded thoughtfully. "Good point."

"Then…" Derek gestured with his glass, gaining hope

as his proposal gained momentum. "Then, you ask her to move to Phoenix with you."

Joe reacted as if he'd been stung by a bee. "Huh?"

"Well, isn't that what you want?" Derek thumped his glass down on the table.

"Yeah, but…"

"It's what you want. Do it. You don't feel like you have the kind of confidence she wants? Fake it. Eventually it becomes real."

He waited for Joe to process the concepts, enjoying his whiskey. For several seconds Joe appeared stunned, then his face seemed to thaw some. His eyes hardened in determination.

"I'll do it." He slammed his hand on the table. Even though his hair was still sticking up on one side, he seemed to grow from a lost kid into a man right before Derek's eyes. If that didn't impress Sarah, nothing would.

"Good. Good for you. I bet you won't regret it." God he hoped not.

"I'll do it. I'll do it right now." He struggled to his feet and then had to sit heavily back down.

"Uh." Derek held up his hand. "I'd wait until tomorrow. Maybe after the wedding, in case things get…emotional."

"You're right." Joe grimaced. "Besides, I probably smell like a distillery."

"Could be." Derek pushed Joe's water toward him. "I'd switch to the soft stuff now. Make your plan tonight. Tomorrow you'll be in much better shape."

"God, if this works, Derek…" Joe laughed nervously. "You'll have made me the happiest guy on the planet."

"Wait, you two are getting married?" Paul walked into the room and grabbed a bottle of water from the refrigerator. "That'll make tomorrow a *really* big day."

"No. No. Not him." Joe put both hands up. "I want to marry your sister."

"Yeah?" Paul grinned and took a sip of water, clearly not surprised by the news. "I was just in her room talking to her. She's pretty bummed."

"Because I'm leaving?" Joe asked hopefully.

"That would be a big fat yes."

"See?" Derek gestured to Joe, then to Paul. "Hey, Paul, tell us how you feel getting married."

"Oh, good, is this my groom interview?" Paul pulled out a chair and sank into it, pretended his water bottle was a microphone. "Well, I'll tell you how I feel, Derek. Ellen is the best woman I've ever met and really right for me, so I guess that means I feel pretty freaking great. In spite of the fact that I can't sleep."

"Nervous about marrying her?" Joe asked.

"No, no, not nervous about the marriage." Paul put the bottle on the table. "Maybe nervous about all the details. Mostly excited about how important the day is to both of us. And also because up in my room lies the mighty Kevin, who snores like an angry yak."

Joe burst out laughing. Derek drained his whiskey glass, thinking of how the story of Paul and Ellen's rocky start might help Joe.

"So you met Ellen and that was that?" Derek knew the answer of course, but when Paul looked at him incredulously, he tipped his head imperceptibly toward Joe.

Paul's face cleared. "Oh, no. I nearly let her get away from me. I didn't, but I still panic sometimes thinking how close I came to messing up my whole life. Just because I was afraid."

"Hear that?" Derek pinned Joe with a meaningful stare. "You know what you want, you gotta stop hanging around feeling defeated and go after it. You want Sarah to go with you next year to Phoenix? Ask her. You have strong feelings for her? You need to…tell…her."

He froze in his chair, feeling as if he'd just kicked himself in the chest.

Holy shit.

"Derek?"

Derek found himself on his feet, gaping at Paul and Joe. He forced himself to focus on his friend's concerned face. "Paul. Was Addie in the room when you were talking to Sarah?"

"No, why?"

"Any idea where she is?"

"No."

Derek was already half out the door. How stupid could he be? Had he told Addie how he felt? Had he told her what he really wanted?

He'd just given Joe the exact advice he needed to hear himself.

ADDIE SAT ON the promontory where she and Derek had walked to watch the sunset his first night on the island. Wednesday night. Today was Friday—or rather the wee hours of Saturday. Three days. It was ridiculous to be feeling that strongly about him so soon, and it was stupid to be sitting out here this late. She should be in bed so she could enjoy Paul and Ellen's wedding the next day without being exhausted. Where was her common sense?

She didn't know. All she knew was that at the moment, she couldn't move. The hypnotic rhythm of the sea, the glittering reflection of even the tiniest crescent moon, the sense of wild wide-openness around her—who wanted to be confined to a cabin, to a bed? If she could, she'd blast off into space and just keep traveling to infinity for all eternity.

No, she wouldn't.

She'd summon Derek here with magic powers she didn't have, and cast a spell to force him to fall in love with her so they could live happily ever after.

If only it was that easy. Her superpower was not the ability to summon hot men; it was being rational and practical. Like this: she knew that the intense feelings she was experiencing right now were simple infatuation, and that they'd pass easily once she was back to her old life, away from this seductive and wonderful-smelling place. And away from Derek.

The rehearsal dinner had been so lovely, the intimacy between Paul and Ellen so beautiful. Watching the way they knew each other inside out and were so looking forward to making the ultimate commitment—the more Addie saw, the more she realized how silly to think she could have fallen for Derek in such a short time. He must have realized it, too. They'd started the evening with longing glances, not ready to show the gang their new status as…what? Not a couple, yet. Lovers, anyway. A concept well demonstrated by Kevin and Carrie, who were practically humping each other into the bonfire.

But over the course of the evening, the tenuous tie that had been formed between Derek and Addie on the private beach started fraying, strand by strand. Their hot looks turned lukewarm, their conversations with people around them intensified. They didn't seek out or spend time alone. Not that there was that much opportunity, except to say good-night.

Such a comedown. But good. The hurt showed her that she was really no good at this wild woman thing. Jumping into a sexual relationship wasn't something she could handle. The sharing of their bodies so soon after meeting had only confused the issue, making her think their feelings were deeper than they were.

But, oh, they had felt so deep. Everything about Derek Bates had been intense from the moment she first said hello to him on the house's front steps. She should have known their lovemaking would seem to engender intimacy so soul-wrenching it put all her other relationships to shame.

So. She'd made a mistake. If they had truly connected that deeply, if their souls really had been…uh, wrenched… that connection would not have eroded a mere hour or two later. They'd be upstairs in his room right now making wrinkles in the sheets.

She stiffened. A rustling through the woods behind her. A light bobbing closer. Someone was coming.

Immediately Addie told herself not to get excited, that it wasn't necessarily *him*. And even if it was, she shouldn't get excited. There were twenty plus people on the island, which made the odds of it being Derek a mere—

"Addie." His deep voice shot thrills through her. *Oh, Addie. Be sensible.* "What are you doing out here so late?"

"Hi, Derek." She turned her head to acknowledge his presence, awareness of him making her skin feel as if it were coming to life, nerve endings reaching for his touch. Shameless little buggers. "I'm sitting here soaking in the atmosphere. I wasn't sleepy."

"It is beautiful." He sat down next to her, turned off his light. Addie held still, every cell in her body screaming at her *not* to be sensible. Hadn't she just told herself her deep reaction and emotional tumult around this man had faded?

Yeah, uh, never mind.

And hadn't she just told herself that those feelings weren't to be trusted anyway?

Uh-huh.

"You okay?"

"Sure." She stared out at the water, annoyed at herself for avoiding a meaningful answer, but what was the point? She wasn't okay, and wouldn't be until she was back home in New York among all her familiar people, places and things and thoughts of Derek had finally left her alone.

He took her hand, lazily stroking up and down her fingers. "We need to talk, Addie."

Nerves burned through her in spite of her being sure there was nothing to say except hey, that was fun, seeya later. She should tell herself instead that it was nice of him at least to want to do that. Many men wouldn't bother. "Okay."

"I don't want to talk here."

"Why not? What's wrong with here? It's beautiful, it's private and it's got a great long drop onto jagged rocks in case I need to push you off."

He laughed and her heart soared with pleasure. *Stop it, Addie.*

"I want to talk to you out on the water in a rowboat under the moonlight." He glanced up at the tocnail clipping of a moon. "What there is of it."

"What?" She turned to gape at his dim shadow. "Are you serious?"

"Yes, why?"

She couldn't believe he had to ask. "It's the middle of the night."

"Yeah…?"

"As in dark."

"Dark, yes."

She gestured toward the water. "*Very* dark."

"It sure is." He squeezed her hand. "Want to go?"

"But…" A giggle was trying to come up her throat. He had the perfect amount of patient amusement in his voice, which had made her listen to herself to find out why he was amused, and to discover that she sounded like a dork. He didn't have to say a word and he got his message across.

Addie didn't want to be a dork.

"It's dead calm. We'll stay close to shore." He got to his feet and held out his hand, his palm a pale invitation in the black night. "Yes?"

She put her hand in his, and let him help pull her to her feet where he held her inches from him for a few charged seconds that had her heart beating up a storm. "Okay."

"Good." Keeping her hand, he turned the flashlight back on and pointed it toward their feet, guiding her safely into the woods and back down to the beach, where *Lucky's* skiff was waiting.

Ten minutes later, Addie couldn't imagine what she thought might have been remotely bad about this idea. The air was cool and fresh, the stillness mesmerizing, the creak and splash of oars a wonderful atmospheric addition. Hard to imagine the vastness of the water they were part of when the darkness made the space feel so intimate. And being with Derek made her so agitated and worked up, but also, very strangely, content. If you could be content while filled with a violent longing for wild sex.

"So." Bumping sounds of wood on wood as Derek stowed the oars. "Let's talk."

"Okay." She sighed. How much better just to keep drifting, away from land, away from troubles and issues and everything that had seemed so important?

"We probably should have had this talk at the beach this afternoon. But we were too busy…being active."

Addie smiled. "Is that what we were doing?"

"And, in my case anyway, being waylaid by emotions

I didn't expect or, frankly, want to have. Which made it hard to sort them out."

Addie held her breath until it occurred to her it would be pretty hard to have a conversation if she wasn't breathing. "What emotions?"

She didn't expect him to answer right away. Or at all, really. It was unfair to ask him to be so vulnerable by exposing his feelings when she hadn't been planning to let out any of what she'd been—

"I feel very strongly about you." He spoke easily, in a steady voice, as if he was telling her he liked her outfit. But the effect on her...thank goodness she was sitting down or she'd have pitched off the boat. *I feel very strongly about you.*

She had no idea what to say. She had to say something. She couldn't leave him hanging out there.

"Oh."

He laughed. "Well, not quite what I'd hoped for, but okay. I'm a patient guy, we have time."

"That's one thing we don't have."

They drifted farther, the white sand beach a barely visible crescent, stars crowding the sky above them, the sliver of moon showing just above the island's treetops.

"It's funny, when we were kids thinking about our futures, even when we were just out of school, didn't it seem as if whatever we did would be under our control? Maybe we wouldn't get the exact job we wanted right away, or the apartment we wanted, but somehow we'd work it so we had it all eventually. No matter which doors we picked, the others would still be open to us if we wanted them to be."

Addie thought about her life and which doors she'd chosen. Always the safe ones, the ones that would take her where she'd already planned to go. She hadn't really considered any other paths. They'd been closed in her mind all along. "I never really wanted too many doors open at once. But I do know what you mean."

"These days every now and then I come up against a door that's locked in my face. I bought *Joie de Vivre* understanding that life with her would be all-consuming. It was and still is what I wanted. But, Addie…" He took a deep breath. "I didn't count on meeting someone like you."

Addie stifled a gasp, feeling torn in half. Part of her was thrilled. He'd said exactly the right thing at exactly the right time, and how often did that happen? And yet… it wasn't the right thing, because there was no point admitting feelings for each other. She didn't want a pen pal for a boyfriend.

"I agree, it would have been nice to have more time together to understand what we started." Addie stopped her speech abruptly, rolling her eyes. Derek had been passionate, sincere and direct, and she sounded like she was talking about developing a new insurance policy. She'd try again, keeping firmly in mind that she had plans to start a new, more interesting and involved life back in New York. This man was not her final and only chance for happiness or personal growth. "Knowing we have to leave this here…is really hard."

"You have no idea how hard."

"Ha." She snorted. "I'm sure you'll be back to women in every port very soon."

"Doubt it." He eased himself off the seat onto a waterproof cushion on the boat's floor and opened his arms. "Because you're the only one I want. Come here?"

"Derek…"

"Yes?"

She sighed heavily. The sensible, rational Addie thing to do was to explain that there was no point in them indulging in any more romance because it would only make it worse when they had to leave each other.

But…Derek must again be bringing out the wild woman in her, because she was finding it very hard to convince herself that sitting here on a cold seat alone was a better idea than sitting in his lap with his warm arms around her.

She pulled herself together and addressed his silhouette. "I don't think it's a good idea for us to touch each other."

"Not a good— Are you *nuts?* It's the best idea I've had all day."

His response was so unexpected she burst out with a nervous giggle. "Derek…"

"I get what you're saying, Addie. I really do. But I need to ask you something, and it would be a big help to hold you while I'm doing it."

Ask her what? Addie stared at his dark form. How could she refuse him? She couldn't. She didn't want to. Relief swept over her as she moved toward him, giving in to what she'd wanted all along, and sat down between his legs on the other half of the cushion.

His strong arms came around her, his chest was broad and warm at her back. He laid his cheek on her hair. She felt sheltered, protected, cared for.

Irresistible.

"So." She'd meant to speak in a no-nonsense tone, but her throat was thick with emotion, and all she managed was a gentle syllable. "What's so frightening that you can't face it alone?"

"My life on *Joie de Vivre.*"

She laughed. "I'd say you've done pretty well alone so far."

"I have." His arms tightened around her. "But I don't want to do it anymore."

Her brain started a tornado of thoughts. Her heart was pounding. *Be sensible, Addie.* He'd met her three days ago. He was not about to do anything crazy, like sell his boat and move to New York.

Was he?

Of course not. She hated when her brain went sailing ahead into unlikely waters.

"I was talking to Joe." His jaw moved against her hair when he spoke. His chest rumbled.

Addie turned her face closer to his, unable to resist the temptation. "About what?"

"I was yelling at him for not taking the risk of coming right out and telling Sarah how he felt about her, and what he wanted and needed from her." He kissed her temple, bent his head to lay his cheek against hers. "And then I realized I was doing the same thing with you."

Addie closed her eyes, struggling to stay calm. "Derek, he and Sarah have known each other for almost ten years."

"Doesn't matter. It's the same deal. If I don't ask you this now then I lose you for sure."

Her argument died. Her heart was hammering, blood hot in her cheeks. Was he going to change his life for her? For *her?* "Ask me what?"

"Addie." He paused, long enough that she nearly started to panic. "I want you to spend the next year on *Joie de Vivre*. Working and living with me."

13

"WHAT?" In Derek's arms, Addie stiffened into an iron statue, exactly as he'd expected her to. *"What?"*

He smiled in the darkness. Anyone would react that way. And, strangely, instead of being in an agony of suspense waiting for her answer, he felt relaxed, freer and happier than he'd felt in a long time. Too long. He hadn't hidden, hadn't closed down and entered the hell of "what if?" He hadn't held himself aloof, gone about his own business and let others do the same. Because he wanted Addie to be his business, and vice versa. What she decided was beyond his control, but he'd gone after what he'd wanted, the same way he'd gone after *Joie de Vivre,* even knowing it would be a long, tough fight.

Until he met Addie, he hadn't recognized how far he'd stepped back from life after getting the boat. Addie had brought him screaming—and shouting and skipping and laughing—back into it. For that he'd always be grateful, even if she fried his heart by turning him down.

"I asked if you'd come live with me on my boat next year."

"You… But I can't just… I mean…" She struggled

to sit up straighter, away from him. "We've known each other three days."

"True." He let the silence hang, listening to her sputter, practically able to hear the wheels turning in her head, knowing he probably came across like a crazy person. "Don't answer now. Just think about it. This might be the change you're looking for in your life, or it might be too much change. We might find we're meant for each other, or we might want to hurl each other overboard after two weeks. I don't know. I just know that I haven't met anyone like you in a long time, maybe ever. I want to find out what's here, and I think maybe you'd like that, too."

"If course I would, but…" She slumped down then straightened again. "Derek. Look, this is really sweet of you, but I can't—"

"Shhh." He pulled her back against him, nuzzling her hair, leaning her to one side to gain access to her beautiful neck. "Don't use reason. Not now."

"Not *now?* Now is the perfect time. There probably won't ever *be* a more perfect time than now."

"Why?" He pressed his lips against the smooth skin under her ear.

"Because…something like this, something this big… We have to be sensible."

"Why?" He slid his hands up her rib cage, stopping just under her breasts, then let his thumbs explore their rounded underside while his mouth explored her throat.

"Because this is a huge, vitally important decision that affects every aspect of our lives, and you can't—" She gasped and arched against his hands, which had moved up to cover her gorgeous breasts. He shifted under her, getting hard. This woman drove him wild. "Um, you can't just… I mean— Will you *stop* that?"

"Why?" He slid his hand under the elastic waistband

of her shorts, and moved between her legs, over the cotton of her panties. She gasped again, but held still, letting him finger her.

"I, um… Oh, hell, there was some reason." She moaned as he lightly stroked back and forth, barely touching her through the thin, soft material. "Derek, you're not playing fair."

"Do you want me to?"

A long sigh. The tiny gurgle of waves against the planks of the boat. The far-off cry of a loon.

"No." She turned her face to his and he took her lips in an explosive kiss that made his erection swell so painfully against her beautiful bottom he was nearly ready to come himself. Somehow he kept his cool, kept up the gentle brushing touches across her cloth-covered clitoris. She was breathing fast, moving in jerky bursts as if it was getting harder to control her body.

She was turning him on like crazy.

"Derek." His name came out a breathless plea. Addie tried to wriggle around to face him, rocking the boat dangerously.

"Shhh. Wait. Hold still."

She obeyed, breath coming in pants, her skin getting damp. Derek returned to torturing her, increasing the pressure and speed of his fingers—but only slightly.

"Derek. *Oh*." Her cry was desperate; her fingers clutched his arms so hard it hurt. He kept her on the edge, stroking slowly, holding her tight against him so she couldn't move from his grasp. *"Please…"*

"I'll make you come. I'll make you come so hard you'll scream. And next year on my boat I'll make you come every day. Every morning, with my tongue between your legs, and every afternoon bent over the seat by the helm, and every night in my bed." He murmured the words into her ear, voice low and passionate, his cock harder than it had ever been in his life. But in spite of the pure eroticism of his words, he felt caveman protective, possessive and oddly tender. He wanted to give her those moments, every day, show her how she was desired, wanted, respected.

And maybe someday more.

Instead of terrifying him, the idea of falling in love added new power and excitement to this time with her. Why else would he want her to move onto his boat? He'd never invited any woman he was dating to do more than experience *Joie de Vivre* for a day or two.

Addie. He gave in, gave her what she wanted, what she needed, slid his fingers underneath the by-now damp cotton and found her clitoris.

She exploded nearly instantly, her body tensing, a long, low cry ripped from her.

He plunged two fingers inside her, feeling her heat, her moisture, the contractions grabbing at him. It took everything he had to keep his own needs under control while she came. He wanted to turn her around, have her straddle him and bury himself in her as deeply as he could go.

As if she read his mind, instead of coming down slowly and savoring her afterglow, she gathered her legs under her. He could feel them trembling. "Addie."

"Shh." She pulled down her shorts then offered him her gorgeous rounded behind.

Derek groaned and yanked open his jeans, jammed on a condom while she waited, keeping his eyes on her beautiful shape, nearly out of his mind with desire.

Protected, he grabbed her hips and positioned her over his vertical cock, which was so eager for her it was jumping and pulsing like a creature with a mind of its own.

Around Addie, he'd started to wonder.

She took hold of his erection with warm fingers, making his breath hiss out between his teeth, then, using her strong thigh muscles to keep herself up and balanced, she lowered herself onto him.

Almost.

He could feel the hot entrance to her vagina nudging the tip of his erection.

Oh, no. Payback for the way he'd made her wait for her climax. He tried to thrust higher, but she straightened, lifting herself so his cock stayed only that tantalizing inch inside her no matter how far he strained.

"Addie, you don't understand."

"No?"

"See, it's okay for me to tease you. But you need to give me what I need when I need it."

"Ahhh, really." She started manipulating her body, squeezing, releasing, squeezing, releasing.

"Addie." His teeth clenched. Sweat gathered at his hairline.

He might not survive this.

"Ye-e-s?" She swiveled her ass in a gloriously sexy circle, taking his cock on the ride of its life. Then, she sank an inch lower, pulled back up immediately. Did it again.

Too slow, too shallow. He wanted to come *now.*

And yet. This was elegant, sensual torture like he'd never had before, even more intense than on the beach, and the part of him that wasn't ready to scream was enjoying it—and Addie—very, very much.

He wanted her with him next year, all year, every day of it.

Another inch, another, then she froze, held still with him halfway home. She could probably feel the impatient jumps of his penis inside her. Derek waited as long as he could, ragged breathing betraying his true state.

"Addie. Have mercy."

"Like you did on me?"

"Well, eventually…"

She laughed and half twisted her upper torso, started playing with her breasts for his benefit—or detriment as the case might be—pushing them up in a sublime offering, drawing her palms across the nipples, letting her head drop back with the pleasure she was giving herself.

That was it.

He took hold of her waist and pushed her firmly down on top of him, letting out a hoarse sigh at the tight, slick feel of her around him. All of him. Finally.

"Derek!"

He ignored her outrage, lifted and dropped her, pushed and pulled, thrusting his hips up and down, making her have to steady herself by grabbing the gunwales of the boat, her head bouncing, moans showing her own pleasure.

His orgasm didn't wait long. He lost control in a few more seconds, pumped her savagely, and came in a huge burst that made his mouth open in a long, silent yell.

Holy moly.

It was a few moments before he could move again.

"Addie."

"Yes?" Her tone was soft, tender, sweet. He lifted her off him, cringing with regret when he slid out, a regret that was swiftly over when he pulled her back against him, wrapped his arms tightly around her, even knowing their time was nearly over, wanting to keep her close.

She wouldn't move to be with him on *Joie de Vivre*. Why would she? She had a job, an apartment, a whole life. It was completely absurd for him even to entertain hope that she'd give it up for him.

And yet…if he'd let huge odds keep him from trying, he wouldn't be a yacht owner at all.

"What would you say if I asked you again, Addie?"

She laughed, relaxed and warm against him. "This answer wouldn't count."

"No?"

"No. Sexually induced slavery is not a fair bargaining tool."

He grinned. "I'm pretty sure the slavery goes both ways here."

"Derek." She was serious this time. "I have a job."

"I know."

"An apartment."

"Yes."

"It's not like I can just leave."

"No."

"I mean…" She gestured in exasperation. "Jobs aren't exactly a dime a dozen."

"Right. I understand."

"And rent-controlled apartments are even rarer."

"Got it."

"Besides, I'm thinking—"

"Come on, Addie. Are you trying to convince me or yourself?"

She giggled in his arms, and he felt a powerful piercing sweetness in his heart that could only be one thing. He loved her. It had happened, much sooner than he thought after meeting her, much later in life than he expected. So he was capable of the emotion, he just hadn't been in the right place at the right time with the right person. And now, he'd fallen within a few days of knowing Addie, as if his capacity for love had been hiding in the wings his whole life waiting impatiently for him to get it right, and now couldn't wait to let him know he had.

"Right now I'd do anything you asked me to."

"Yeah?" He pretended to think it over. "How about swimming over to that island and picking me some—"

"Except that."

He laughed and kissed her, then kissed her again, and since it didn't seem as if there could possibly be anything more wonderful in the world to do, he settled in to kissing her, tasting her mouth over and over, holding her warmth to him, immersing himself in their cocoon of intimacy in this tiny boat on this vast, dark ocean.

"Jobs can be put on hold," he whispered. "Apartments can be sublet."

"I know. But..." She sighed, running her fingers down and across his arms in a gentle caress. "I'm just not the kind of person who can make such a huge decision on the spur of the moment. Honestly, I wish I was. It's tempting, it sounds as if it would be incredibly exciting. I certainly feel closer to you than I should after such a short time, but it's just... Well, it's completely crazy."

"You're right. No question."

"When I was a girl, my parents taught my brother and me that there was a right way to do everything. A right way to speak and behave and eat and dress and wash... right programs to watch on TV, the right people to know. Everything was so black and white for them, everything was so carefully worked out. My brother rebelled in a big way. He spent his whole life doing as much wrong as possible. Drugs, women, dropping out of college to wander around the world, making just enough money at whatever job he could find in order to take him to the next country and the next job, making friends with the lowest of the low, in short rejecting everything they taught us."

Derek chuckled. "He sounds like someone I'd like to meet."

"He's great. He really is. I admired his rebellion as much as I was appalled by it. I bought into my parents' version of life because I was so shy that any form of rebellion would have plunged me into anxiety and panic." She twisted around to peer up into his face, though neither of them could see much. "Do you see what I'm saying? If I said to hell with it, I'll come with you, it would probably destroy us, Derek. I'd be a complete wreck away from everything I know and feel safe around."

He wanted to point out that she'd changed her life several times already. Going to college, moving to New York, that life on a boat wasn't nearly as foreign as she probably imagined. That after a few weeks that life would start seeming normal and everyday as well, full of the same dull moments and repetition and routine as any.

But instead he gave her a final squeeze, understanding that he'd get no further tonight. It was beyond late and they were both exhausted. He'd back off and enjoy Addie tomorrow at the wedding, then ask her once more Saturday night and then again Sunday morning before they left if he had to.

"I understand, Addie." He kissed her lightly. "Want to go in? Big day tomorrow."

"We probably should." She moved out of his arms regretfully and sat in silence on the row back to Storness.

At the top of the hill the house was dark and quiet. Derek led the way in and to the bottom of the stairs, and then gave Addie one last kiss, guessing neither of them would sleep much during what was left of the night.

But as he said good-night and watched her walk through the living room to the bedroom she shared with Sarah, his arms and body itching for the feel of her, he knew that even if his hopes of returning to the *Joie de Vivre* with her beside him were obliterated this weekend, he'd still find some way, any way, that they could be together again.

Because having found a woman like Addie Sewell, he was not going to settle for anyone else.

14

PAUL AND ELLEN's wedding day dawned sunny and clear. Well…it had *probably* dawned that way. Dawn happened during the one or two hours of sleep Addie managed to get before the household was up and working, taking down tents and cleaning and closing up the house. Right now Addie was carrying a load of borrowed sleeping bags down to the beach so *Lucky* could transport them back to the mainland.

The previous night, she'd dragged herself away from Derek's warm arms and kisses to lie awake in tense bewilderment over the enormous decision he'd handed her. Of course her practical side thought the idea of ditching everything she knew to follow a near stranger out to sea was completely ridiculous, and that she'd never allow herself to do such a thing. That side of her was cranky and exhausted by the turmoil and change and utterly unpredictable nature of the past several days. That side of her wanted to climb onto a plane and go home, get a solid night's sleep and wake to peace and blissful routine, and not give crazy ideas another moment's consideration, because what was the point of torturing herself pretending there was a decision to be made? There was no decision. The answer was clear.

But…

The side of her that had recently been awakened, that had just started to tune into all the things she'd been missing since she was a girl, carefully scheduled out of any control of her own life and decisions by well-meaning parents who saw themselves merely as guides, not tyrants—that side, which was only just starting to be tired of always playing it safe, was tempted enough to want to keep the options alive, to keep more than one door open, as Derek had put it last night. That side, so long deprived, was now hungry. The beast had awakened. It wanted to make up for years of hibernation, to explore and indulge these new and powerful feelings, to shake up her life and for once do something completely irresponsible and totally unlike herself.

But…

This was not the way she would have preferred to awaken that beast. She would rather it awoke bit by bit, comfortably, leisurely, getting used to each stage of awakening before it progressed to the next. Small risks? Like finding new and exciting places and ways to seduce Derek? Yes, yes, bring them on. Risk finding herself out of a job and an apartment, floating around in a new life she could turn out to hate with a man she might not ultimately be compatible with? That was like being woken from a deep sleep because your house exploded around you.

So…

Maybe there was a compromise? Some way to indulge her new hunger for change—and for Derek—without completely abandoning the woman she'd always been? She could visit him in Hawaii, or wherever he happened to be, and go along on a short cruise to wherever he was scheduled to go. He could visit her in New York. They could meet somewhere in between.

But…

If they really wanted to test the viability of their relationship, long-distance with only occasional passionate too-short reunions was hardly the way to go about it. Addie was nearly thirty, she wanted to settle down, and who knew when or if Derek would ever be able to do that.

And yet…

Addie groaned. She'd been going around and around on this for the past twelve hours. That morning, she'd seen Derek, but apart from a warm smile and a surreptitious hand-squeeze, there had been no chance to mention the importance of their possibly life-changing discussion the previous night. All of which left her feeling it had not been quite real, and that maybe she was angsting for no reason.

"You okay?" Ellen fell into step beside her on the path to the beach.

"Oh." Addie gave an embarrassed laugh. Apparently she'd made her frustration audible. "No, it's fine. Just… a lot on my mind."

"Hmm." They crossed the sand and handed over their bundles to the crew working to load the skiff. "Tell you what. Let's take a break."

"Really?" Addie gestured back toward the house. "There's still a lot to do."

"We have plenty of people working and plenty of time. The ceremony's not till four."

Addie looked doubtfully at the line of burdened wedding guests approaching *Lucky,* reminding her of a colony of ants. "I'd feel bad if we didn't—"

"Ahem." Ellen crossed her arms across her chest. "I'm the bride, and I get to decide."

Addie giggled and curtseyed meekly. "Yes, ma'am."

"C'mon, let's go." She took Addie's arm companionably and led the way back up the hill toward the house, turning left onto a narrow trail Addie had noticed before but never followed. "Have you been down here? It's one of my favorite spots."

A few dozen yards later they emerged from the trees onto a part of the island dominated by great granite ledges that sloped into high tide, which, along with a good breeze, was sending waves crashing into shore, causing spectacular eruptions of white, foamy spray.

"Ellen, this is wonderful."

"Come on." Ellen strode out onto a section of ledge near a large crevice in which small stones had collected; a gift from the power of the sea.

"I love to sit up here and chuck rocks in the water. It's crazy but fun. Good stress relief, too. Want to?"

"Sure." Addie couldn't say stone-throwing tempted her that much, but this was Ellen's parade and she wasn't going to rain on any of it.

"Wait up here, I'll climb down and get us a bunch." Ellen scooted down, leaping the last few feet and landing with a clacking crunch at the bottom of the crevice. A minute later she reemerged, grinning triumphantly, bulging pockets making her hoodie sag midthigh. "Got 'em."

"Good haul." Addie gave her a thumbs-up, still feeling uneasy about ditching work, wondering what Derek was up to.

"Have a seat. I'll divide them up."

Addie wiggled around until she found a place that fit, and accepted a lapful of assorted size rocks, smoothed and rounded by constant tumbling.

"Now." Ellen sat, picked up a stone from her supply and hurled it. A second later, the most delightfully liquid *thwunk* and splash made them both laugh for no particular reason.

Addie took her turn. Another *thwunk,* more splash, strangely and wonderfully satisfying.

"Okay." Ellen consigned her next one to the deep and smoothed her hair, which the breeze promptly messed up again. "I have a confession."

"What's that?" Addie threw another rock, farther this time, enjoying the release.

"I used to be really jealous of you." Ellen tossed one high in the air.

"What?" Addie was so astonished she didn't watch for it to come down. "Of *me?* What on earth for? You've got everything."

"Paul was in love with you for years."

Addie's jaw dropped. She laughed uncertainly. "With *me?* Paul? No, no, he wasn't. Not with me. You're confusing me with someone else. We hung out together all the time as friends. With Sarah and Kevin and a lot of others. It wasn't me."

"Yup, it was." Ellen threw her next stone, then wiped her hands together, that's that. "He was absolutely crazy about you. You were his perfect woman."

"But…but that's impossible." She laughed again, incredulous rather than amused, mind racing back over their grade school years, remembering parties, movies, board game tournaments, softball and soccer and tons of plain old hanging out, trying to see now what she must have been blind to then. "He never said anything. Showed anything."

"Lucky for me."

"No, no, Ellen. I would never have—" She broke off, not sure if it was polite to tell someone you found the love of her life sexually unattractive. "I mean Paul is like a brother to me. Always has been."

"He knew that. That's why he never told you."

Addie anxiously studied Ellen's profile. Her voice and expression were unconcerned, but sometimes people could hide bitterness. Addie didn't sense any, thank God. "Wow. That is just so…weird. I never picked up on a thing."

"No. You didn't." She said the words with unusual weight, which made Addie feel a bit anxious again, and unsure how to respond.

A heron flapped over, its wingspan impressive after so many gulls and cormorants. A crow gave a guttural croak from the trees behind them, as if annoyed at the intrusion into its air space.

Addie found herself tensing again, undoing the relaxation their rock-throwing session had started. She was beginning to think Ellen had some motive bringing her here besides Bride's Prerogative to avoid work.

"Did Paul ever tell you how we got together?"

"You met on a blind date, took one look at each other and that was that."

Ellen threw another stone, watched it splash. "That's the version for public consumption. It was more complicated, and more difficult."

Addie felt a jab of disappointment. She'd loved the idea that the two of them had found true love simply, honestly and easily. Did it ever happen that way? "Complicated how?"

"Paul fought how he felt for a long time."

"No." Addie was too flabbergasted to throw her next stone. "But it's so obvious you're perfect for each other."

"Mmm-hmm." Ellen arched an eyebrow at Addie, who was clearly being sent some signal, but had no idea what it meant. "However, it wasn't obvious to him, not at first.

He'd wedged himself into this narrow mindset about who he was and about his feelings for you. He wasn't really open to me, even though he thought he was ready for a relationship, and had been dating around looking for one."

Addie pelted the water with two rocks at once, hard, as if she was punishing them. "How did you convince him?"

Ellen nudged her, blond bob fluttering around a mischievous expression. "Take a wild guess."

"Ha!" Addie's grin stretched her mouth to its maximum. "I'm shocked. *Shocked,* I tell you!"

"I knew you would be." Ellen waggled her brows lasciviously before settling back into being serious. "But that wasn't the whole story of course. One day he told me that before he could commit to me, he had to tell you how he felt about you. He thought that was the only way to finally put those feelings to rest."

"Urgh." Addie cringed, waving away Paul's imaginary speech like a bad smell. "That would have been so painful all around. For him, for me, for you…"

"I didn't know how it would go." Ellen shrugged, gazing distantly out to sea. "I was only sure of how I felt about Paul, and how I was pretty sure he felt about me underneath, and that I'd have to fight to keep him for both our sakes. So I told him if he didn't stop hedging and making excuses, in short, if he wasn't *man* enough to give us a serious shot, I was outta there."

"Really? You would have left him?" Addie gasped, horrified to think that this perfect couple might not have made it as far as this weekend's joyous celebration. Then she caught a look in Ellen's eyes. "You were bluffing."

"Of course I was bluffing!"

Addie burst out laughing. She liked Ellen more and more. "But Paul didn't know that."

"Exactly." She heaved a larger rock over the ledge and

nodded in grim satisfaction at the splash. "I gave him the ultimatum Friday, left him alone all weekend and caught up with him Sunday night. He was a wreck. Absolute mess. But he jumped, and I caught him like I said I would."

"Thank God he did."

"The point of all this is, Addie." She turned and fixed Addie with a look that made Addie brace herself. "We both took a risk for something we not only believed in but deeply wanted to happen."

Addie narrowed her eyes. Okay. She was getting it now. Someone had been talking to someone about certain decisions involving big risks. "Gee, Ellen, is there any particular reason you happen to be telling me this now?"

"Who, me?" Ellen plonked a hand to her chest, eyes innocently wide. "No, of course not. Just a bride musing on her wedding day."

"Uh-huh." Addie picked up a good-size rock, heart beating like mad, not sure what she was feeling. "Has someone mentioned something about me and a certain, oh, I don't know, other person lately? Anything?"

"No, no, not at all." Ellen spoke reassuringly. Addie didn't buy it for a second. "I have really good intuition about this stuff. You and Derek have been setting off sparks since you met. I thought maybe y'all needed a push in the right direction."

"Ha." Addie hurled the rock as hard as she could. "I wouldn't begin to know what the right direction is."

"Addie, all I know is that the only two people who walk on water in Paul's world are you and Derek."

"And you."

"Well, *obviously.*" She winked.

"Me, I was in the water yesterday." Addie mimed a sudden drop. "I sank right to the bottom."

"Don't sell yourself short. You were really important

to Paul, his first ideal of love. And Derek was kind of his savior. My life with Paul wouldn't have been possible without Derek. The close relationship Paul has with his family would not have been possible without Derek. Any kids we have would not have been possible without Derek. He is a good, good person who has had a lonely and hard life, and he needs someone really wonderful who can..." She frowned and gestured aimlessly. "I don't know—"

"*Rescue* him?"

Ellen laughed. "That's about the last word I'd think of when it comes to Derek, but I suppose there is an element of that. Anyway, I'm just saying, Addie, that sometimes we need shaking out of our usual ideas about ourselves and what we want and deserve in life."

Addie pressed her lips together, suddenly annoyed by all the talking around the issues. "Can we just be blunt here?"

"*Yes.*" Ellen spoke with exaggerated relief. "Thank you. I would love to be blunt."

"I permit you to be blunt. What exactly are you saying?"

Ellen sat up on her haunches and put her hand on Addie's shoulder, her lovely blue gaze earnest and warm. "I think you should give Derek a chance next year. Give him a sense of home. I don't think he's ever had a real one."

A jolt of adrenaline, a burst of joy, then, predictably... fear. Damn it. She was sick to death of being afraid.

"Wait a second." Addie pointed accusingly when Ellen's words sank in. "Give him a chance next year? That is *way* past what you can know by intuition. Even really good intuition."

"Okay, okay." Ellen captured Addie's finger. "Put away the weapon, I'll squeal. Derek and Paul talked last night and again this morning. I'm playing meddling match-maker. That's it."

Addie blew on her finger and holstered it. "You should never work for the CIA."

"Cracked like an egg, I know." She gestured to Addie to throw her last stone and stood. "Now, sugar, having delivered my supersecret spy message, I am going back to help. You coming?"

"Absolutely." Her stone made it farther than anything she'd ever thrown in her life, fueled by giddy adrenaline and a growing certainty.

The story of Paul and how he'd nearly blown the chance of forever happiness with Ellen affected Addie deeply. Fear had ruled her for far too long. Fear of the unknown. Fear of what could happen. Both were imagined negatives, neither were real threats.

Her feelings were real. Derek's feelings were real. His offer to see where those feelings could lead was real.

And she might just have to accept it.

THE WEDDING WAS the most beautiful thing Sarah had ever seen. It didn't hurt that she was already imagining hers to Joe. Because of course that was their next step. The Brisbanes' house was a majestic white Victorian with sage trim, built by a ship's captain in the mid-nineteenth century at the height of the region's prosperity. It sat on a lovely sloping lawn with a spectacular flower garden, where the ceremony was held, designed to make the most of Maine's short summer season—gladiolas were in full bloom in a riot of colors, black-eyed Susans and daylilies grew in profusion. Tables had been set up for the reception around the lawn, which had an expansive view of Machias Bay. The band was playing on the front patio next to a floor set up for dancing. The weather had been perfect.

Mr. Brisbane, Esq., had officiated at the ceremony, since lawyers were permitted to marry couples in the state of Maine. He'd spoken warmly of the couple, of their devotion to each other and to their families, had cautioned Paul and Ellen to be good to one other above all else, and generally reduced Sarah and many other guests to mushy sniffles, which got louder and more obvious when the couple recited vows they'd written themselves, gazing rapturously into each other's eyes. Sarah couldn't be happier for her brother and her new sister-in-law. The reception had been joyous, food and champagne plentiful, the dancing and socializing enthusiastic.

But now it was time for her.

From where she'd been standing next to the bride during the ceremony, Sarah hadn't been able to see Joe, but she could sense him behind her in one of the chairs set up for the guests, imagined that maybe he was watching her, too, that maybe he was thinking about them being up at an altar in front of an officiant reciting their own vows.

Maybe. She hoped.

The day had gone by in a blur. Sarah had done everything she could to treat Joe the same as usual, so her at-last declaration would be a surprise. And in case her certainty about how she felt about him waned, which it decidedly hadn't. Once she'd finally admitted her feelings to herself, Joe had changed permanently into the more masculine, more handsome man she'd only caught glimpses of before. Frankly she'd had trouble keeping her hands off him. Just the idea of what she'd say and do to him tonight—soon!— had her shivering and hot at the same time.

Now, at last, the moment she'd been so impatient for and so nervous about was here. Paul and Ellen had left a few minutes earlier, the guests were starting to clear out and she was happy to say that Derek and Addie had left together soon after the happy couple. Sarah so hoped they'd work out. Why she ever thought Kevin would be right for Addie, she had no idea. Why she'd thought half the stuff she'd used to, she had no idea, either. Too much of her life had been spent in a weird distorting fog. Finally she was starting to see things—and herself—clearly.

If only she could see clearly how the rest of this evening would go. She knew Joe had feelings for her, had for a long time, but maybe he'd gotten to the end of his rope as she'd just gotten to the beginning of hers. Maybe he'd trust that she'd had a true change of heart. Maybe he wouldn't. Sarah couldn't blame him either way. All she could do now was put her plan into motion and hope for the best.

She scanned the thinning crowd until she found Joe, chatting with one of Paul's friends next to the dance floor. Even her hundredth or so glimpse of him this evening thrilled her. They'd spent most of the afternoon apart— Sarah had maid of honor duties and she was terrified she'd give something away if she spent too much time with him. Joe could read her like a Nook.

Okay, Sarah. Ready, set, go.

She moved onto the dance floor and caught the eye of the bandleader, who nodded.

Now.

Squaring her shoulders, Sarah made a beeline for Joe. By the time she was next to him, the band had started her request, the last song of the evening, "It's Your Love" by Tim McGraw, which he performed with his wife, Faith Hill.

"Dance with me?" She caught Joe's hand and tugged him onto the floor, where a few brave couples had stuck it out nearly to the bitter end.

"I hate dancing."

"So?" She turned to face him, standing close, and put

her arms around his neck, aware of his tall, solid body in a way she'd never been before. "It's the last song, you can manage one."

"I don't know, Sarah."

She rolled her eyes, heart pounding, same old teasing Sarah, and yet she felt so different, so much more of a woman around him, so much calmer and more sure about who she was and what she wanted. "You can handle a slow dance. Even my two-left-feet brother can handle a slow dance. And frankly, if there's anyone who needs to be afraid right now, it's me."

His deep brown eyes had been avoiding hers. At this, he looked down at her. "You? You're a great dancer."

"It's not the dancing I'm afraid of." She started swaying, aware of the song's romantic lyrics flowing around them, the warmth of his body close to hers, the way it drew her. How could she have been so stupid for so long? Joe...

"So?" His hands remained stubbornly at his side, though he made some attempt to move with her. Not wildly graceful, but not embarrassing, either. He was a fine dancer. "What are you afraid of?"

"The dance being over. The weekend being over. You leaving me."

His mouth pressed in a line. A muscle twitched in his jaw. How had she never noticed its strength? "I'm taking a new job, not leaving you."

"Joe?"

"What?"

"Put your arms around me."

"Sarah..."

She moved closer, pressed against him. "Please, Joe."

She felt rather than heard him sigh. Then his arms came around her, reluctant at first, then firm and protective, and for the first time in her life held by a man she wanted, Sarah felt absolutely safe and absolutely content. "Thank you."

"You're welcome." He was grumpy as a bear. She ignored him and pressed her cheek to his—as far up as she could reach. His scent was so clean and masculine, his skin so just-shaven smooth, the song so romantic and beautiful. She couldn't let his mood undermine her resolve.

"Joe?"

"Yes." His tone was slightly less exasperated. Maybe she was getting to him? She hoped so. Because it was time.

She tightened her arms around his neck, pressed her forehead under his chin, unable to meet his eyes. "How about I move with you to Phoenix?"

His body stiffened. "Right."

"I'm serious, Joe."

"Why the hell would you move to Phoenix?"

"Because you'll be there." She summoned all her courage and looked up, letting her feelings show in her face. *I love you, Joe.*

His brows drew down. "What are you playing at, Sarah?"

Ouch. She kept her features from sliding into dismay, told herself to be patient. He was going to have to accept a radical change after a decade of everything being the same. It would take more than a few minutes for him to trust her. "I'm not playing. I want to be with you."

Silence for a few minutes while he searched her face. "I don't understand what you're saying."

"I'm saying…" She stopped dancing, stayed still in his arms and looked him full in the eyes while hers filled with tears. "I'm saying I love you, Joe. I want to be with you, wherever you are."

The band swelled into the final chorus. Joe didn't move.

Sarah started to feel a bit panicky. She told herself to calm down, but it wasn't working very well. "I love you."

"So you said."

"I thought…that's what you wanted from me." Panic for real this time. What if he'd only loved her for all this time because she was unreachable? What if he'd been doing the same thing Sarah had been doing for so long with guys like Kevin and Ethan and Derek?

What if he didn't really want her?

"Where is this coming from, Sarah?"

"My heart." More tears. She couldn't help it. Joy and fear together.

Still no movement, still the stoniest of stone faces.

"Joe, for God's sake." Okay, she was never going to be patient. She could only change so much.

He glanced around. The band had stopped. The guests that hadn't already left were doing so now. "We need to talk about this somewhere else."

"Yes. Okay." She took a deep breath. This could still work. "My room at the hotel."

It took Joe a few seconds to agree. The instant he did, she practically dragged him off the dance floor, over to thank the Brisbanes, and down their yard to her car, which she drove like a demon to the hotel where they were spending the night, wishing they could be back on Storness, on the beach under the stars, wishing she'd had the brains and timing to seduce him there.

But her room at the Machias Motor Inn would have to do.

She let them into her second-floor room with the view of the Machias River, and tossed her bag on the bed, kicked off her shoes and faced Joe, who was standing uneasily next to the bed. She put her hands to his chest. "Let's try this again?"

He shook his head, bemused, adorable, dark hair tumbling over his forehead. "Sarah, you are confusing the hell out of me."

"It's very simple. I'm telling you I'm in love with you."

He dropped his forehead into his palm and groaned. "Since when?"

"Since I figured it out."

"Just now?" His looked up suspiciously. "Right after watching your brother get married? After several glasses of champagne?"

"No." Tears rose. She pushed away from him. "No. Yesterday, when we were talking, when you told me you were leaving. I realized I can't live without you."

"That is nothing like—"

"No." She held up her hand to stop him. "That's not what I meant. I *can* live without you. But I don't *want* to live without you. You've been such a vital part of my life for so long, my very best friend. I'm so sorry I put you through so much, and I'm so sorry it took me this long to realize what you mean to me."

"A best friend?" His voice cracked hopefully and she realized what this was costing him. The rest of her life wouldn't be long enough to make it up to him, but she was damned if she wasn't going to try.

"So far your best friend. But from now on…" She stood very still, understanding what must happen to make what she was saying clear. Words wouldn't be enough to convince him.

She reached behind her neck, found the zipper on her dress and pulled it down.

Joe's eyes widened, then his face turned stony again, hands fisted at his side.

Her dress slid to the floor. Underneath she wore a lacy white bra with matching panties and thigh-high stockings.

"Sarah…"

"Yes, Joe?" she whispered.

"I don't…" He took a step forward, then stopped, his expression finally showing emotion. Want, fear, love, fear, desire…fear. Sarah's heart melted. *Oh, Joe.*

"I've been so slow. So selfish." She unhooked her bra, let it slide off her arms, conscious of her breasts in the cool room air. "So blind."

He blinked. Swallowed, staring into her eyes, glancing down at her body as if he couldn't help himself. Then the ghost of a smile. "Thank God I'm not."

Sarah grinned, hope shooting up inside her like a geyser. That was her Joe. He had come back to life, snapped out of whatever zombie state she'd put him in. Maybe this would be okay. Maybe not too little too late.

Down came her panties. She kept the stockings on, sauntered toward him, helped him take off his jacket. "I have a favor to ask you."

He made a sound she'd take as an appropriate response.

She put her lips near his ear, loosening his tie. "I want you to kiss me, Joe. Then I want you to make love to me until I beg for mercy."

He shook his head as if to clear his brain of fog. "I still can't take this in. I don't—"

"Shh. Don't worry. We'll take it slowly." She threw the tie across the room, put her arms around his neck and pulled his face down, kissed his mouth.

Deep desire spread through her. She understood desire. She was used to desire. What she wasn't used to was the sweet depth of emotion she felt along with it.

Joe.

She kissed him again, more deeply this time. His eyes stayed closed, his hands at his side, but his mouth moved, responded.

Then a low groan began in his chest and he enveloped her in a crushing embrace, kissing her as if he'd never wanted to do anything else. The sweetness grew and spread, and with it, hot desire she felt him return from a certain place that for men was a dead giveaway.

"Sarah." He repeated her name over and over between kisses, sliding his hands up and down her arms, over her back.

She backed up, smiling into his eyes with everything she felt for him, with all her hopes for their future together. In Phoenix or wherever else Joe was. That was where she belonged.

"Where are we going?" He was smiling now, and she knew it was sinking in, that he was starting to trust what she felt, and that the next hour spent in this motel room would be the final proof he needed.

She climbed onto the bed, lay back, inviting him to join her. "We're going to make my wish on the shooting star come true."

Joe climbed reverently onto the bed with her, wearing way too many clothes, but they would soon take care of that. He moved over her, pressed his forehead to her forehead, his heart to her heart.

"Trust me, Sarah. Both our wishes will come true tonight."

15

ADDIE GAVE A LONG, joyous whoop and ran down the riverbank behind the Machias Motor Inn, not caring that her panty hose probably wouldn't survive the trip. Her heels, she'd left in Derek's car and who cared about them, either? If she fell, her sleeveless blue silk sheath would be toast, as well. Too bad! She was happy! Incredibly happy! The wedding had been amazing, Paul and Ellen were going to be blissful the rest of their lives and she'd all but decided to chuck her entire existence and spend the next year on the yacht of a particularly hot guy named Derek Bates.

Arms came around her waist and lifted her, shrieking with laughter, spun her around, then deposited her back on terra firma. Terra mostly firma—she hadn't been shy with the champagne and the world seemed to be tilting ju-u-ust the tiniest bit.

"Mmm." She kissed Derek's most *ama*-zingly awesome lips and threw her arms around his neck, breathing hard from her run. "That was the best wedding I'd ever been to."

"It was pretty special." He was looking at her funny. Was she being funny? She didn't think so.

"They're going to be together forever, I really feel it. Really. I'm serious."

He nodded, looking totally hot in his gray summer suit. She couldn't wait to see him in his yacht captain outfit. She'd bet he looked incredibly hot in that. And naked? She already knew what he looked like naked: amazingly hot. Face it, the guy was hot.

"Sometimes, like this one time I went to a wedding and I just knew the marriage wasn't going to last." Her voice was coming out too high. That was weird. She tried to pitch it lower. "And it didn't. Well, it did for a year, and then *pthhhhhpt.*"

"Yeah?" He was definitely amused now, but just as she was about to ask him what was so funny, he lunged forward and picked her up, swung her around and around again, and kissed her the way she'd always dreamed about being kissed, which come to think about it, was pretty much the way he always kissed her.

Really, he was perfect.

"I could happily suck face with you forever, Captain Bates."

"That's a pretty long time." His eyes were warm, his smile wide.

"It is, isn't it." She kissed him again, then pressed her body against him and turned the kisses slow and suggestive. "You know what?"

"Mmm, what?" He slid his big warm hands over her bottom and pulled her roughly closer, grinning down at her.

"We've never had sex in a bed."

"You're right." He quirked an eyebrow. "Though I would have been happy to the first night when you shamelessly crawled into mine."

"Mistakenly. Only it didn't turn out to be a mistake."

Addie smiled up at him. She hoped that night would never seem like one. Or any of the time she'd spent with him.

"I think deep down you knew it was me."

"Very possible." She batted her eyelashes and slid her hands under his jacket, savoring the firm curves of his pectorals. "So I'm thinking we really need to make love in a bed."

"That sounds—"

"Now!" She broke away and ran back toward the hotel, giggling madly. She felt so free tonight! So wild! She couldn't remember when she'd had this much energy, this much savage adrenalinc. This much joy. Her life was about to change in a huge way, a significant way, and so was she! Gone was the drudge, gone the creature of habit, gone the slave to routines and predictable safety. She was... Neo-Addie!

It felt so damn wonderful.

Thudding steps sounded behind her. She picked up her pace, knowing he could catch her casily if he wanted to, but why not make him work harder?

He let her reach the door of their room half a second before he did, though she didn't have a key, so what good had the sprint done her except give her a chance to enjoy the joyful rush of air into her lungs, the pull of her muscles working hard, the fabulous feeling of being an alive and mobile and feeling woman who was madly in love with a wonderful man and about to declare she'd spend the next year carefree and pampered aboard a luxury yacht. A yacht! Captained by the sexiest man alive, ever.

While Derek opened the door, she assisted by wrapping her leg around his and helping herself to the enticing muscular feel of his back under his jacket, hungry to get him alone and naked. Did she mention naked?

Inside, she threw herself into his arms and kissed him,

backed him up toward the bed, conveniently located as
the centerpiece of the room. She couldn't wait. The wedding had been so lovely, so very lovely, and while she'd
loved every second of watching Paul and Ellen seal their
happiness, the evil selfish part of Addie had just been
craving *this*.

He tumbled her back on the bed, held her wrists over
her head and covered her body with his. Oh, yes. He
wanted the same thing she did. Bodies joined and writh-
ing in—

"Addie."

"Mmm?" She moved her hips in a circle under him,
smiling, glorying in the feeling of being pinned down by
a strong man. "Can I help you, sir?"

"We need a time-out here."

"A what? Why? What are you talking about?" Her voice
crept back up too high, and became strangely brittle.

"Shh. Just lie there for a minute. Take deep breaths."

"What? *What!*" She laughed at him. "I don't need to
calm down. I'm in a great mood, that's all."

"Shh." He brushed his lips across hers. "Breathe."

Addie rolled her eyes, and obediently tried to slow her
breathing.

It didn't work. Her lungs stuttered and fought. She
started to feel a bit light-headed, a bit panicky. What was
the matter with her? How did he know?

"Turn over." He released her hands, turned her over
and unzipped her dress, pulled it off her shoulders and
unhooked her bra.

Oh, yes. Forget breathing, now they were getting somewhere.

She waited impatiently for him to finish undressing
her, for his hands to slide under her breasts, for his body

weight on top of her, for the nudge of his erection searching for her opening from behind.

Instead his hands landed on her back and began stroking, top to bottom, bottom to top, following her muscles, his touch light at first, then increasing in pressure. Slowly, sensually, he massaged her. She lay waiting, unsure of what was happening, wanting to know when he'd turn this sexual.

"Relax, Addie." He started on the long muscles next to her spine, smoothing them, spending time on the knots, one inch at a time, kneading and loosening. Then her deltoids, her upper back, around her shoulder blades—light strokes, then deeper, singling out muscles and insisting they let go. On and on he worked until her breathing became even and deep without her trying. Her eyes closed, her world dwindled to his touch and the wonderful sensations in her body. She hadn't realized how much tension she'd been carrying until he decided it had to go.

"Better?" His stroking became light again; he drew the tips of his fingers over the skin on her back, covering every inch, then laid his hand in the center and pressed gently.

Addie was nowhere near where she'd been only half an hour before. She felt as if she'd gained ten pounds. Her body would leave an Addie-shaped crater in the mattress that would never rebound. But…very strangely, her heart and spirits had sunk down from their high, first to normal, and then into an odd free fall she didn't want to examine just then.

"Thank you," she mumbled. "That was wonderful."

"You're welcome." He pressed a kiss to her shoulder.

"Except I don't think I'll ever be able to move again."

"Darn." He kissed the small of her back, the top of

each buttock, then nudged her legs open, burrowed his face down and kissed between them.

Addie's eyes shot open, her dismay dissolving. "Um…"

"Yes?" His tongue joined in what his lips had started.

"Well…" She inched her legs farther apart. "Maybe I can move a little."

"Mmm." He took advantage of the new space she'd given him. His tongue was very warm and very wet and she was getting very, very hot in spite of the near stupor he'd put her in. She responded to him so strongly. It wasn't just his tongue, it was the reverent way he tasted her, the brush of his hand on her thigh, the small murmurs here and there that let her know he was making love to her as a whole woman even while touching only one special part.

A minute later he stopped and Addie felt him leave the bed. The sound of clothes being removed got one of her eyes open again. She rolled over to watch him, heart still strangely heavy.

Tie first. Derek tugged it off with practiced ease and tossed it onto the room's chair. Shoes and socks next—he took care of those standing on one foot without over-balancing. Trousers. Addie nodded appreciatively as his strong, muscular thighs came into view. Shirt unbuttoned, off. T-shirt. Off. His chest was broad and defined without being over-pumped. His abs ditto, a muscular washboard she wanted to drag herself over repeatedly.

Boxers off, and her man was naked, putting on a condom, climbing back onto the bed. She reached for him. "Welcome back."

"Nice to be back." He positioned himself over her, stroking her hair, gazing into her eyes. Addie's heart rose to meet him. It had no choice.

Then Derek kissed her, over and over again, softly, sweetly, firm lips exploring and tasting. Addie felt the last of her giddy wildness leaving, replaced by deep emotions that both filled and frightened her.

He reached down to prepare her then slid inside, taking his time, pushing in slowly. When he'd buried his last inch, he paused. Looking into his eyes she felt the most powerful connection she'd ever known, and out of that bliss, out of that loving, wonderful certainty, came understanding of a deeper, painful truth that she'd soon have to face.

He began to move, slow thrusts, slow retreats, pausing in between. Her arousal grew sharply, but he held his pace and she lay still, letting him take the lead, running her hands over the smooth firmness of his back, tracing the rounded muscle of his buttocks, cupping the hard swells of his shoulders, biceps and triceps, indulging every sensation, keeping her mind carefully blank.

Tomorrow would happen tomorrow. They still had all of tonight.

Derek didn't seem to be in a hurry, either. He took time to kiss her mouth, her temple, to bend and suckle her breasts, adoring her nipples, the tugs of his tongue and lips, the rasp of his stubble against her skin increasing the sensation and her arousal.

Out and back in, pushing to the hilt, moving his hips in a circle pressed tightly against her clitoris, then back out, and back in, a lovely, leisurely rhythm that kept her desire burning hot, but not yet desperate.

She explored the soft, thick texture of his hair, drew her fingers down the planes of his face, tasted and tested every angle and aspect of his mouth.

"I could get used to this," he whispered. "I'd like to get used to this, Addie."

No, no. Not now.

She could tell the truth, that she'd like to get used to

this, too, but he might think that meant she'd decided to go with him, and she couldn't tell him that.

So she pulled his mouth down passionately, kissed him as if it were the last time. He responded with equal passion, and that passion translated into the language of their bodies and made them move urgently against one another as if, again, it might be the very last time.

Addie went over first, holding Derek tight, arching back into the pillow, mouth open, holding stone-still through the rush of ecstasy, so he'd feel her contracting around him, so he'd know what he'd done for her.

He drew in a sharp breath, exhaled, *oh, Addie,* and plunged deep into her, hands dug in under her buttocks to merge them more closely. In and out only a few more times, then he stiffened, moaned low, and she felt him pulsing inside her, reveling in his climax with a rush of tenderness that nearly undid her.

They came down slowly. Instead of a flush of triumph, she felt a deep sadness, wrapped her arms around him and pressed her cheek against his, feeling his breath warm her shoulder.

One minutes, two minutes, she wasn't sure how long they lay there until he lifted and met her eyes, his dark with sadness. "You're not coming with me."

Addie shook her head.

"Tell me why."

"I can't handle that much change, that much risk. I was going to. I'd gotten myself all excited, all ready. I was going to tell you tonight. You saw what it did to me." She paused, determined not to cry. "I was a totally manic wreck. If it was the right thing to do, I'd be able to tell you my decision calmly. Instead I nearly fell apart."

"I sensed that." His eyes were full of pain, but also understanding, which made it even harder not to cry.

"I would love to find out what could be between us, Derek." Her voice broke. "Maybe there's another way. I mean…we can keep in touch. You could visit maybe, or I could."

"Sure." He kissed her gently, but she knew what he was thinking, because she was thinking the same thing. They might stay in touch, might retain some of the passion for a while, but without contact, without access to each other, there was nothing solid they could build. To get to know someone enough to maintain a relationship, to make any kind of commitment, there had to be something other than occasional passionate reunions. They could go on that way for years, in a limbo of impermanence.

Addie didn't want that. She wanted a man she could get to know intimately over many, many months, his moods and his routines, to face trials and joys together, discover each other's secrets and strengths, wonders and weaknesses. She couldn't do that with a man half a world away.

Derek pulled carefully out of her, disposed of the condom in the room's little bathroom and brought back glasses of water for each of them.

She watched him move, that glorious body, well-balanced and graceful, muscles flexing and contracting. He climbed back into bed and pulled her close. Addie sighed heavily. "I'm in total ridiculous denial how much this is going to hurt."

He chuckled, that deep glorious sound that was going to tear her in half every time she remembered it for the next several weeks. Maybe months. "I think we both are."

"But it's time to put on my big-girl pants and deal with reality." A tear slipped past her defenses.

"I guess it is." He wiped it carefully off her cheek and kissed her, kissed her again, sweetly, reverently. Her heart was breaking. She was surprised not to hear it cracking in her chest.

"When do you head out to sea again?"

"Thursday. I'm taking a group out of Lahaina Harbor on a three-island tour."

Addie nodded. She'd be going to the office. Sitting at her usual desk, interacting with her usual colleagues, going home to her usual apartment.

It was what she wanted. What she needed. It was her chosen life.

"After that?"

He frowned, thinking. "After that a fishing trip. Then a birthday cruise."

She'd still be going to the office.

But maybe by then she'd have enrolled in a class, met new people, broadened her horizons, interests and skills. Not the same in-a-rut-Addie, but not trying to be her polar opposite, either. Something in between. Something she could handle without losing her mind.

She lay in Derek's arms, head on his chest, legs tangled with his, thinking she'd never felt so blissfully relaxed with anyone. But if she'd discovered this now with him, it must mean she could do so again, right? Derek wasn't the only man she could find happiness with. And because he was so wonderful, he'd raised the bar for her. She wouldn't settle for ho-hum relationships again. That was another check in the plus column. Silver linings. After the worst of the pain subsided, she'd find more of them. She was certain.

Eventually she dozed, woke to find Derek stroking her awake, drowsy at first, then, wow, um…very, very awake.

"Addie," he whispered. "Wake up."

"I'm up. It's not morning."

"No. But I'm thinking since we might not be able to make love again, at least for a while…"

"Ah. Good thinking, Captain Bates." She rolled him onto his back and straddled him, holding his arms to the mattress, the way he'd imprisoned her earlier. "I agree with you. We'll make this a good time."

"A night to remember."

"Uh." Addie frowned. "Isn't that the name of the book about the Titanic disaster?"

"Could be."

"I'm not sure that's appropriate for what we're planning."

"Sure it is." He struggled up and flipped her over, making a mockery of her physical dominance. "How about this. 'As captain of the ship, it is my duty to go down.'"

Addie burst into laughter, loving that he could make her smile, even through this dense cloud of misery. Her laughter cut off in a gasp as his mouth found her between her legs.

Fear entered her heart at the same time pleasure spread through her body. Yes, Derek had raised that bar.

But what if he'd raised it to a height only he could ever attain?

16

THE SOUND OF the ocean woke Addie. She was back in Derek's arms, listening to waves tumble over rocks on the shore outside their window. A seagull laughed nearby.

Addie's eyes shot open. Registered the familiar white ceiling.

"Alarm off."

The ocean was not outside her window. Derek was on the other side of the world. There *were* birds calling, but they were pigeons on the roof of the Russian Orthodox Church opposite her apartment building, making that deep gurgle noise in their throats, as if they were forever using mouthwash. She missed the wild free call of gulls, eagles and osprey, the thrush and other songbirds. She missed the ocean and its wonderful smells. She missed Derek something fierce.

Leaving him three days earlier had been one of the hardest things she'd ever had to do. Addie preferred relationships neatly wrapped up when they ended, with literal or figurative notes of apology, regret, thanks or sympathy dutifully composed if not sent. This was a mess of loose ends, full of doubts and what-ifs. And yet, she'd stayed true to herself by deciding to come home to New York.

She'd done the right thing for herself and, ultimately, for Derek.

Eventually this ten-ton spiked weight she was carrying around in her heart would dissolve into the satisfaction of exactly that understanding.

She bloody well hoped.

"Time."

"Six fifty-five," Tick replied.

Six fifty-five. The latest she'd figured she could get up without having to rush any of her morning.

Addie dragged herself out of bed, remembering suddenly how the week before she left for Maine she'd been having trouble getting up, too. Funny. She'd been thinking about getting her Vitamin D checked or her iron. And yet, she'd felt fine—more than fine—in Maine. Plenty of energy, zest for life, you name it.

Just her rut, which she was going to get out of as soon as possible. She'd clean up those boxes of Great-Aunt Grace's and maybe look for a condo for real this weekend. September was right around the corner, there would be classes of all kinds starting soon.

In the meantime, she could get back to the kind of life she needed to keep herself sane.

In the bathroom she counted to seventeen until the shower was warm, scrubbed her hair and body, humming a melody she abruptly stopped when she realized it was Avril Lavigne's missing-you song "When You're Gone."

In her bedroom, she dressed quickly and efficiently in the clothes she'd ironed and laid out the night before.

In her kitchen she fixed and ate the same breakfast she had every morning: a banana, granola with yogurt, a half piece of toast with butter and jam—sometimes honey— orange juice, milk and coffee.

In the subway she read that day's *New York Times,* saving the crossword to do at lunch.

In her office she dealt with the day's tasks from eight-thirty until eleven forty-five when she broke for lunch to beat the rush at the cafeteria and secure her favorite table.

In the cafeteria, with the crossword section under her arm, she selected carrot sticks, a sandwich, an apple and skim milk to be sure she was getting enough calcium.

On her way to her usual table, sitting empty waiting for her, Addie came to an abrupt stop, nearly causing the woman behind her to dump her tray contents down Addie's back.

Her routines were not comforting today, as they had been the first day back, and then a little less yesterday. Today they were stifling her.

"Addie?"

She turned to find Linda Persson back at *her* usual table, with *her* usual lunch. Linda must have been sick Monday and Tuesday. Or maybe she'd decided to take a trip after all.

"Hi, Linda, welcome back. Were you out on vacation this week?" She could hear the hope in her voice, not sure why she'd care either way.

"No, no, I was out sick. Nothing serious. I'm much better now. How was Maine?"

"Wonderful. The wedding was lovely. It's good to be home, though." Sort of. For the most part. In spite of being bored and having a huge jagged hole in her heart. She took a step toward her regular table then hesitated, struck by inspiration. If anyone could make her feel good about her decision to forgo a life of constant uncertainty for a life of total stability, it was Linda. "Hey, can I join you?"

Pleasure lit Linda's face, making Addie feel guilty for wanting to have lunch with her for such a selfish reason.

"Absolutely, come on over. I'm dying to know what you thought of Maine. My friend Marcy and I are thinking of going there."

Addie set down her tray and took a seat. "Really going there?"

"Well, yes." Linda seemed surprised Addie would ask. "One of our friends from college opened a B&B outside of Portland and invited us. So I want to hear all about your trip."

"I thought you didn't like to travel."

Linda looked trapped, and then gave an embarrassed shrug. "That was partly sour grapes. I had no reason to go anywhere and it felt terrible. I'm excited about this, though, so tell me everything."

"The state is beautiful, so wild and pristine and free. At least where we were, in Downeast Maine. The seafood is delicious and so cheap compared to the city. It's the kind of place that changes you." Her voice thickened. She bit into a carrot and chewed viciously. "But I'll tell you, after a week of constant socializing I was pretty fried."

"Oh, I bet." Linda nodded. "Weddings are exhausting. But so romantic."

"Yes." Addie picked up her sandwich, trying to look nonchalant, and pretty sure she was failing big-time. "I actually met someone."

"You're *kidding!*" Linda spoke so loudly a couple of people turned to look.

"No, I'm serious." Addie was a little annoyed. Was it *that* incredible to think she might have met a guy? "A friend of the groom, who's an old friend of mine."

"Weddings are great places to meet people. All that love in the air." Linda leaned across the table, eyes hungry. "Tell me about him. Does he live close by? Is he from Maine? Will you see him again?"

"Well, actually…" Addie leaned in, too. She wanted this to have maximum impact, to enjoy Linda's shock and dismay. "He asked me to leave New York and live with him."

"Oh, my *gosh!*" she yelped. More people turned to look. "After a week? Where is he from? What does he do?"

"He's a charter yacht captain. Based in Hawaii."

Linda gasped so hard she started choking on her sandwich, and had to hold her hand up to tell Addie to wait, and then drink water a few times. "Oh. My. *God.* You have to tell me *everything.*"

Addie told her the short version, leaving out the part about Kevin and climbing into Derek's bed by mistake, though her whole body was remembering that part so vividly she kept leaving bits out of the story and having to backtrack. Linda, either very polite or totally enraptured, hung on to every word. Addie told her how Derek had taken her to watch the sunset, how he'd shown up to surprise her when she was sunbathing privately—Addie left out naked—how he'd taken her on a moonlit rowboat ride and danced with her by a river under the stars.

And then how after only three full days, he'd asked her to give up her job, her apartment, her well-ordered life, and follow him out onto the ocean to go who-knew-where for who-knew-how-long, who-knew-when.

Crazy, right?

Silence as Linda stared at her in horror and sympathy. Slowly, slowly, the pain in Addie's stomach started to lift. Here was someone who'd understand. Someone who'd be able to tell Addie to her face that she'd done the right thing. Sarah thought Addie was nuts. Ellen thought Addie was nuts. Paul thought Addie was nuts.

Linda would understand.

"Are you *nuts?*"

Addie was so shocked she sat there with a carrot stick halfway up to her mouth.

"You came back *here?*" Linda gestured around the cafeteria. "Instead of living on a *yacht?* With a guy you were completely *crazy about?* You came back *here?* To *this? This company* and this *cafeteria?* And that *carrot?*"

Her voice became louder with each phrase. Her face turned bright red. Around them people were falling silent. By the time she said "carrot" she was practically shouting.

Addie managed to put the carrot down.

"Yes," she whispered.

Linda looked around, noticed people staring and lowered her voice. "Will he still take you?"

Addie's eyes shot wide. "No. I mean I don't know, but no, I can't go. I'm not the type of person who can just up and leave everything I've built for myself. I can't handle huge changes like that. And boats…I don't think it's for me."

"Oh, so you mean last time you tried living with an amazing hunk on a yacht you didn't like it?"

"I never said he was an amazing hunk."

"Is he?"

"Well…" Addie wrinkled her nose. "Yes. But that's not the point."

"Agreed. The point is that you are nuts. Boats have schedules, too, they have to, to function smoothly. And after you've been on it for a while the life will become second nature like anything else. How long has this guy been at it, you think he's enthralled with every new day, with every aspect of his job?"

"I guess not."

"But he wants to be enthralled every new day. With you, Addie." She shook her head slowly, eyes narrowed. "And you said no."

Addie could only sit and blink at her.

"Go." Linda was whispering. "Go now. Just walk right out of here. Tell you what… I'll take care of your paperwork. We can give you whatever, vacation time, sick time, short-term disability, you leave that to me. If you go and change your mind in the first month or so, you'll still have a job to come back to. I'm sure you can manage your rent for a few months. But for God's sake, don't let this pass you by."

"Why are you doing this for me?"

"Because I had an offer like this. From a military man. We'd known each other a short time, but we were crazy about each other. Before he went abroad, he asked me to marry him. I was a timid homebody and panicked at the idea of living overseas, of moving whenever the military said we had to. I couldn't handle it. I've regretted that every day because no one I met after him came close. That was my chance. That was my life calling me, Addie, and I ignored it because I didn't give myself credit for being able to evolve into more than I already was. I know now I could have handled it. And if I couldn't, I could have left him, older and wiser. But this way I'll never know. And there is no greater hell to live through than that." Her eyes filled with tears. She slammed her fist onto the table. "Go to him. Right now."

"Linda, I—"

She stopped Addie with an upraised hand.

"Go now. Before you change your mind. Trust me. Go." She leaned forward and took Addie's hand, looked earnestly into her eyes. "Do not even finish your carrot."

DEREK STOOD AT the helm of *Joie de Vivre,* having steered carefully out of the tiny Lahaina Harbor on Maui. He was heading northwest with his six passengers to explore the island of Molokai. This was one of his favorite trips, a full eleven days, with the passengers designing the itinerary. After Molokai, this group wanted to visit Lanai, then Hawaii. Usually he was in great spirits at the start of a trip, and today the weather was glorious: eighty-two degrees with full sun and calm water.

It might as well have been forty degrees with dense fog and towering seas.

Up until the minute he started *Joie de Vivre's* engines, he'd been hoping Addie would change her mind. Eleven days from then he was sure he'd still be hoping. Hell, next *year* he'd still be hoping. His bookkeeper, Mary, was due to go on maternity leave after they got back and he'd made arrangements to hire a temp rather than give up hope Addie would want the job.

He and Addie had agreed to keep in touch, but his last email on Wednesday morning had gone unanswered for four days. Four miserable minute-by-minute days. Derek had considered calling, but pride kept him from the phone. Addie knew he still wanted her, knew he still wanted to hear from her, still wanted her here with him. He wasn't going to beg.

Most likely.

Derek closed his eyes briefly against the pain, shaking his head. Listen to him. He missed her so deeply it was as if mini construction workers were hard at work 24/7 jackhammering his heart. Addie had turned him from the cool untouchable captain of his own soul into an obsessed pining wimp.

"Captain." The voice of Renard, his first mate, came from over his left shoulder. Derek hadn't heard him approach.

"Yes, Renard." Derek pulled himself up tall. Apparently he'd even started slumping. By tomorrow he'd probably have developed a permanent whine and half his teeth and hair would fall out.

She was killing him.

"Trouble down in your cabin, sir."

"In my cabin?"

"Trouble with a passenger. Jenny found her when she was cleaning, asleep in your bed."

Derek's mood blackened further. He knew exactly which passenger. The stacked blonde who'd gotten drunk at the welcome onboard dinner the night before and tried to fondle him under the table while her older husband sat right next to her, too wasted to notice.

Lovely people.

"Gene can handle her." His excursion leader was expert at dealing with difficult personalities.

"I've never seen him stopped by anyone before, sir. He claims this is something only you can manage."

Derek's lips tightened. This was ridiculous. "Unless her life is in some kind of danger, there is no reason he can't—"

"I'm…afraid it is, sir."

Derek stared at Renard incredulously. "Her life is in danger?"

"Uh. No, not really." The smaller man's dark eyes flicked to one side, then returned to his. Derek had the distinct impression Renard was amused, and it pissed him off further. "Thing is, sir, she insists on seeing you."

"Right." Derek nodded curtly, wanting to growl. Stupid diva theatrics. "Take the wheel."

"Yes, sir."

Derek banged through the bridge door, thudded down the narrow wood stairs, attempting a smile at one of the passengers making her way to the top deck. Once on the main deck, he strode to the captain's quarters, located in the bow of the ship.

At his door he hesitated, listening. No voices. Gene was nowhere to be found. Damn it. He shouldn't be leaving his captain to deal with this woman alone. Unless there were witnesses, whatever happened would be her word against his.

He knocked. "Hello?"

"Yes?" The voice was strangely high, oddly false sounding. The woman last night had a low smoker's voice. Was she trying to disguise it? "Is that Captain Derek?"

Captain Derek? "This is Captain Bates, what are you doing in my cabin?"

"Waiting for you." The caricature of a voice took on a breathy quality, probably meant to be seductive.

"Ma'am, there are plenty of other places on the ship where we can talk privately if you need to."

"*Talking* wasn't what I had in mind."

Derek rubbed his jaw. There was something very weird about this. Was one of his crew playing a trick on him? They knew better than to risk their jobs or the boat on a prank while their captain should be at the helm. He'd been through all the passengers in his mind, and besides the crazed smoker lady and her husband, there was a honeymooning couple and an older pair celebrating their retirement.

So who the *hell* was—

A thought occurred to him.

A beautiful, wonderful, fabulous thought.

He tested the brass door handle. Unlocked. He pushed it open. Went inside.

Addie.

Naked.

In his bed.

Derek was there in two steps, grabbing her to him, holding her, feeling her warmth, hearing her laugh at first, then dissolve into a couple of sobs he could tell she was struggling to control.

He kissed her. Her hair, her temple, the dimple in her cheek, then he found her mouth in a kiss that lit fires all the way through his body, and cemented her already strong hold on his heart.

He meant to talk to her, meant to discuss the situation, ask how long she was there for, whether she was really going to give their relationship a serious chance or if this was just a short visit.

But she was naked. In his bed. Kissing him as if she really, really meant it, and he was only human and definitely a man.

So in a very short time, his clothes were off and he'd joined her between the soft sheets, reveling in her skin against his, her mouth on his chest, on his neck, his hands stroking every part of her he could reach.

And when he moved over her beautiful body and entered her, they stared into each other's eyes in awe of what was between them, then reached hungrily toward each other and kissed as if they'd never stop, while their bodies heated and mated and made sounds of satisfaction and of deep forever-after love.

He rolled to one side to touch her clitoris, loving the noises she made, the sharp breaths, the gasps, the way her head writhed on his pillow. And when he knew she was close, when a flush covered her body and cheeks, he plunged back into her, sending her over an edge he fell over himself only a few seconds later.

Eventually...very eventually, the movement of the boat reminded him who and where he was. Captain Bates. On duty.

But Addie was with him.

"I can't believe you're here." He nuzzled her neck, inhaling her sweet scent.

"I can hardly believe it, either." She stroked his hair,

gazing up at him, starry-eyed, the most enchanting sight he'd ever seen. "I wasn't going to."

"That part I knew." He took her hand and covered his heart. "Leaving you nearly killed me."

"I know. I kept telling myself the pain would get better, that I'd done the right thing. And then life in New York, which I thought I needed, started to feel like a prison without you."

He couldn't believe he was hearing his over-and-over again fantasy, directly from her lips this time. "You quit your job? Left your apartment?"

"I didn't quit exactly. Not yet. I took vacation, sick time and a short leave. I have a few months to see how this goes." She wrinkled her nose self-consciously. "You know I'm not a risk taker."

"You were smart. We don't really know how we're going to do." He kissed her again, tasting the exquisite corner of her lips, the sweet roundness of her chin, as sure that they were right together as he'd been of anything in his life. That he belonged on the sea. That he was meant to own *Joie de Vivre*. "Though I'm giving us good odds."

"That's my job." She stretched against him, nearly making him hard again. He had a feeling he'd have to change his schedule for the first week or so, in order to include as much lovemaking as possible. "Speaking of which, is Mary's job still open or will I be your kept woman?"

"Her leave starts after this trip. So she'll have time to show you the ropes."

"Well, Mr. Captain. I've been reading about boat stuff. We sailors call them 'lines,' not 'ropes.'"

"Is that right?" He drew his finger down her full soft lips. "I can see you have a lot to teach me."

"I should think so."

He grinned, so overwhelmed by emotion he could hardly speak. "I'm so glad you're here, Addie."

"So you can get laid regularly?" Her eyes told him she was teasing, but he wondered if she knew.

"So I can tell you in person that I love you."

Surprise widened those eyes then emotion filled them with tears. "Oh, Derek."

"Too soon?"

"Would I be here if I thought you were a passing fling?"

He grinned. He would have liked to hear *I love you, too,* but her eyes were telling him loud and clear. His cautious woman could take all the time she needed. "Listen, I better call my crew and let them know I'm being unavoidably detained."

"They couldn't have been nicer to me. Paul called Renard and vouched for me, so they let me sneak on."

"Totally against ship's protocol."

"I should have asked you?"

He kissed her, getting hard again, thinking he'd give them about three months of sea-time bliss before he started shopping for an engagement ring. "Only the captain can give you permission to come aboard, Miss Sewell."

She turned to lie facing him, draped her leg over his hip and pressed herself intimately against his growing erection. "I'd like very much to come on board, Captain Bates. Then I'd like to come again. And again after that."

"Permission granted." He cupped her face in his hands, realizing that this boat he'd loved for so long had changed with Addie a part of her.

Now she very much felt like home.

* * * * *

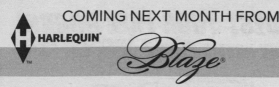

Available August 20, 2013

#763 THE CLOSER • *Men Out of Uniform*
by Rhonda Nelson

Former ranger Griff Wicklow mastered the art of removing a woman's bra in high school, but protecting one worth two million dollars is another matter altogether. Especially when the real gem is the jeweler along for the ride....

#764 MISSION: SEDUCTION • *Uniformly Hot!*
by Candace Havens

Battle-scarred marine Rafe McCawley is in need of relaxation, but when he meets gorgeous pro surfer Kelly Callahan in Fiji, resting is the last thing on his mind!

#765 MYSTERY DATE
by Crystal Green

A woman craving sensual adventure. A lover who hides his identity in the shadows. An erotic interlude that takes each of them farther than they've ever dared to go....

#766 THE DEVIL SHE KNOWS
by Kira Sinclair

One incredible night with a mysterious bad boy in a red silk mask—that's all Willow Portis wants. Too bad she doesn't recognize her devil until it's too late....

HBCNM0813

REQUEST YOUR FREE BOOKS!
2 FREE NOVELS PLUS 2 FREE GIFTS!

HARLEQUIN *Blaze*®

red-hot reads!

YES! Please send me 2 FREE Harlequin® Blaze™ novels and my 2 FREE gifts (gifts are worth about $10). After receiving them, if I don't wish to receive any more books, I can return the shipping statement marked "cancel." If I don't cancel, I will receive 4 brand-new novels every month and be billed just $4.74 per book in the U.S. or $4.96 per book in Canada. That's a savings of at least 14% off the cover price. It's quite a bargain. Shipping and handling is just 50¢ per book in the U.S. and 75¢ per book in Canada.* I understand that accepting the 2 free books and gifts places me under no obligation to buy anything. I can always return a shipment and cancel at any time. Even if I never buy another book, the two free books and gifts are mine to keep forever.

150/350 HDN F4WC

Name	(PLEASE PRINT)	
Address		Apt. #
City	State/Prov.	Zip/Postal Code

Signature (if under 18, a parent or guardian must sign)

Mail to the **Harlequin® Reader Service:**
IN U.S.A.: P.O. Box 1867, Buffalo, NY 14240-1867
IN CANADA: P.O. Box 609, Fort Erie, Ontario L2A 5X3

Want to try two free books from another line?
Call 1-800-873-8635 or visit www.ReaderService.com.

* Terms and prices subject to change without notice. Prices do not include applicable taxes. Sales tax applicable in N.Y. Canadian residents will be charged applicable taxes. Offer not valid in Quebec. This offer is limited to one order per household. Not valid for current subscribers to Harlequin Blaze books. All orders subject to credit approval. Credit or debit balances in a customer's account(s) may be offset by any other outstanding balance owed by or to the customer. Please allow 4 to 6 weeks for delivery. Offer available while quantities last.

Your Privacy—The Harlequin® Reader Service is committed to protecting your privacy. Our Privacy Policy is available online at www.ReaderService.com or upon request from the Harlequin Reader Service.

We make a portion of our mailing list available to reputable third parties that offer products we believe may interest you. If you prefer that we not exchange your name with third parties, or if you wish to clarify or modify your communication preferences, please visit us at www.ReaderService.com/consumerchoice or write to us at Harlequin Reader Service Preference Service, P.O. Box 9062, Buffalo, NY 14269. Include your complete name and address.

HB13R2

SPECIAL EXCERPT FROM

 HARLEQUIN®

 *Blaze*®

Enjoy this sneak peek at

Mission: Seduction

by Candace Havens, part of the
Uniformly Hot! series from Harlequin Blaze

Available August 20, 2013,
wherever Harlequin Books are sold.

"I'm a pro." Kelly laughed. "I surf professionally. At least, I did until a few months ago when I hit Pause and bought this place."

If she'd earned enough to afford this luxury resort, she must have done well as an athlete.

Rafe chastised himself for staring at her, but stopping wasn't an option. He searched his brain to remember what they'd been talking about. "Why'd you hit Pause?"

"To reevaluate, decide what to do next with my life. Burnouts happen and to be honest, I was heading that way. I forgot my love for surfing and I wanted to remember why I've been so dedicated for so long. And it's helped. I can't wait for my next meet." She pursed her lips. "Listen to me. I sound like some weirdo trying to find herself."

"No, you don't," Rafe said quickly. "I love being a marine, but there are days I want to give it up and be a farmer or something."

She grinned. Her amusement pleased him. "You don't seem like the farmer type."

"That *would* be funny, since I've never been on a farm before," he admitted. "But, you know, a job where you work with your hands and you're alone out in nature. No one's giving orders, and you don't have to constantly watch your back."

That was true. After his last assignment, he'd begun to reevaluate what was important to him. Unlike Kelly, he had no idea what might be next. His friend's private security company was his safety net.

But Rafe seldom took the safe path. His beat-up leg was proof of that.

"How did you end up here? Seems like a lot for one person to take on."

"I was always visiting during my time off because the waves are so great. A friend of mine owned it. One day he said he wanted to sell Last Resort, and everything fell into place so easily that I knew it was the right decision. It's a lot of work, but manageable for the most part.

He studied her for a moment. She was proud of what she'd accomplished, and she should be. From what he'd seen so far, this was about as close to paradise as one could get.

"So, dinner?"

"Oh, thanks for reminding me." She grabbed her board from where it'd been standing and tucked it under her arm. "Starts at seven, and it's very casual. Well, see ya tonight." She swung away with a jaunty lift to her step.

His gaze locked on her bikini-clad body sprinting up the beach. The woman was insanely beautiful in a doesn't-need-any-makeup, girl-next-door sort of way. It wasn't fair.

He laughed.

What was paradise without a little temptation?

Pick up MISSION: SEDUCTION by Candace Havens, available August 20, 2013, wherever you buy Harlequin® Blaze® books.

Heaven help her...

Willow Portis tries extra hard to be the good
girl of Sweetheart, South Carolina. But the night
of the Fall Masquerade, she steps out of her
well-behaved shoes and into a supersexy
angel costume. And when she's tempted by
a stranger, she gives in! Too bad she doesn't
recognize her devil until it's too late...

Pick up

The Devil She Knows

by *Kira Sinclair,*
available August 20, 2013,
wherever you buy Harlequin Blaze books.

A hot, new
Men Out of Uniform
story!

Ranger Security has just assigned former
Ranger Griff Wicklow to protect a priceless
diamond-encrusted bra. And while Griff has more
experience removing bras than protecting them,
his job is about to get even more complicated.
Because Temptation just walked in disguised as
Jessalyn Rossi, the drop-dead delectable jeweler
who's going along for the ride...

Pick up

The Closer

by *Rhonda Nelson,*
available August 20, 2013,
wherever you buy Harlequin Blaze books.

HARLEQUIN®

A *Romance* FOR EVERY MOOD™

**Stay up-to-date on all your
romance-reading news with the
Harlequin Shopping Guide,
featuring bestselling authors, exciting new
miniseries, books to watch and more!**

The newest issue will be delivered right to you
with our compliments! There are 4 each year.

Signing up is easy.

EMAIL

ShoppingGuide@Harlequin.ca

WRITE TO US

HARLEQUIN BOOKS
Attention: Customer Service Department
P.O. Box 9057, Buffalo, NY 14269-9057

OR PHONE

1-800-873-8635 in the United States
1-888-343-9777 in Canada

Please allow 4-6 weeks for delivery of the first issue by mail.